BILLIONAIRE BLISS

A NOVEL

SHEILA MURDOCK

It's a Chance of a Lifetime
Her life is about to change forever
But at a cost
Liz Green is just about done with relationships. Coming off of a five-year relationship that ended in a mutual split, she still feels she needs time to herself to focus on what is the utmost important to her . . . being happy once again.
But Liz has no idea just how much her life is going to change when she meets Jeff Vick, a man she never thought in a million years she would meet who is looking for love, and this is the start of a whole new world for her she never thought she would be in, and a world some don't think she belongs in.
She also notices a pattern with Jeff when it comes to getting certain phone calls and texts, and it's not a pattern she likes at all. But it's not long before she starts receiving some unexplained texts of her own from someone who is trying whatever they can to sabotage what she and Jeff are building on their road to ultimate happiness.
HE'S SINGLE AND LOOKING FOR LOVE
Billionaire Bliss
SHE'S SINGLE AND LOOKING FOR HAPPINESS
SHEILA MURDOCK
ALSO AVAILABLE IN PAPERBACK

ALSO BY SHEILA MURDOCK

DIVESTED
Crystal
THE DIVESTED BWWM SERIES
SHEILA MURDOCK
The Vain Society
SHEILA MURDOCK
Entitled Women
SHEILA MURDOCK
LAVONNE ON THE JOB
The Hair Salon
SHEILA MURDOCK
HIS Mess HIS Siren
A NOVEL
SHEILA MURDOCK
LESSONS Lisa
SHEILA MURDOCK
Billionaire Bliss
SHEILA MURDOCK
THE Club
A NOVEL
SHEILA MURDOCK
STANDALONES and STANDALONE SERIES
MORE to COME!

NIGHT SKY AFFAIR: TABITHA IS COMING SOON IN 2024

I'm Sleeping With Your Husband
A NOVEL
WHEN THE UNEXPECTED BECOMES EVEN MORE UNEXPECTED
SHEILA MURDOCK
STANDALONES
MORE to COME!

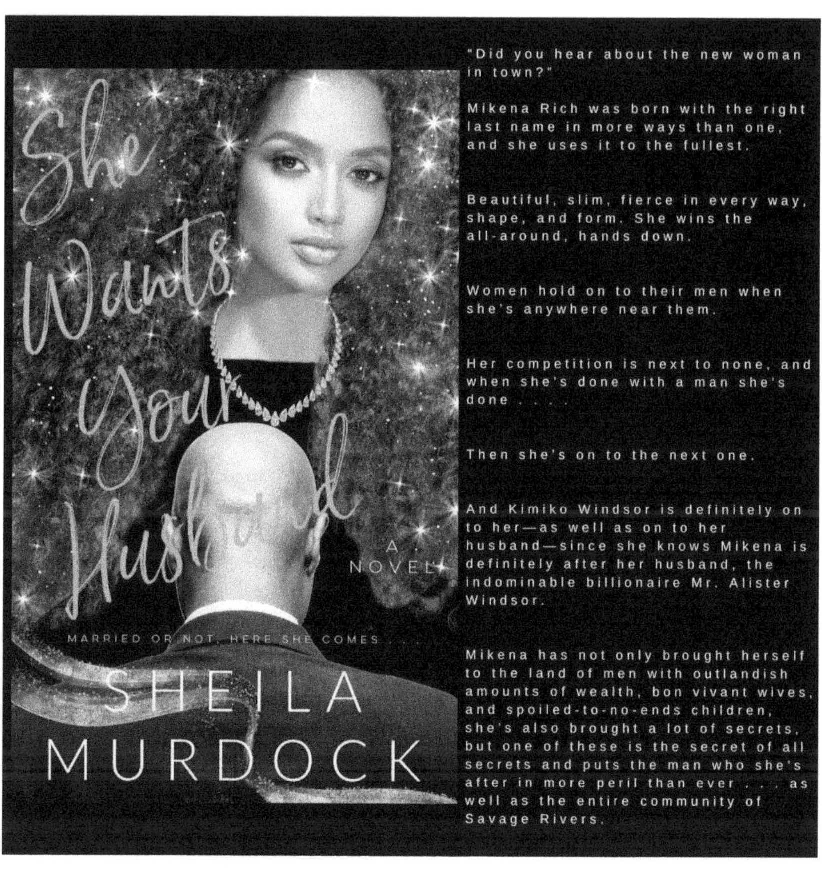

SHE WANTS YOUR HUSBAND - COMING SOON

CHAPTER ONE

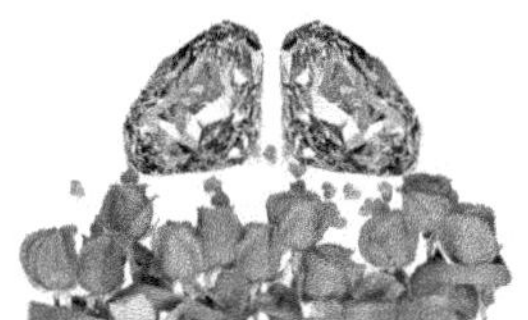

Being at a concert that was dedicated to people being in love was the last concert I wanted to be at, but I was here—front row center—courtesy of my sister Laurel's husband Marlon who was able to snag a third ticket since he got the tickets through the company he worked for. But I felt like the third wheel, in a place where people were in love—or at least they were supposed to be or worse, pretending to be—while artist after artist got up right in front of me and sung a medley of love songs that I just didn't feel like hearing, especially since it'd been only less than a year since my boyfriend Devin and I mutually ended our five-year relationship . . . and he was here tonight with another woman.

I honestly felt like I was the only one not coupled up, with my sister and her husband sitting to the left of me, and a happy-in-love couple sitting to the right of me, who kept kissing every single chance they got. *I swear* they were trying to make me jealous, and any and everything was setting my mind back to what'd happened between Devin and me, and I didn't wanna go there at all because even though we mutually ended it, seeing him here tonight pretty much showed me that he was over me months before we'd ended it, maybe years, but I didn't wanna think about that right at this moment.

I wanted this show to go as fast as it could so I could get out of here and get back home to wallow in an endless pit of junk food and soda, but I knew all that would do was get me to where I knew I didn't wanna be. It was hard enough for me and I didn't need anything complicating my efforts to make myself feel good once again; to be happy once again.

"Liz, are you all right?" Laurel asked me as she held on to her one red rose Marlon got her from a person with a basket full of roses walking around here all night . . . and there were several of them all over the arena. The woman sitting right next to me had one as well from her man. I honestly felt like an outsider.

"I'm fine," I lied. "It's a great show."

It was, but it was not the type of show I felt like I should've been at at this point in my life right now. I knew the thousands of people who were married or had a significant other at this sold-out show weren't all happy, and relationships weren't perfect, but it was something about sitting here all by myself surrounded by couples that may or may not have been in love.

I didn't even know if I still believed in true love and happiness. I thought Devin truly loved me. I thought I truly loved him. I thought we were happy together, but it was clear that after a few years he was never gonna marry me. I was never pushy, never cheated on him, never disrespected him. But he cheated on me therefore disrespecting me and I knew after years of thinking he was gonna change, I truly believed he was waiting for me to take the initiative to mutually end our relationship; he didn't even try to plead with me to give what we knew wasn't there anymore—another chance. He wanted out, and so did I.

End of the show. Finally. I scanned the arena and saw my ex walking down from his seat hand-in-hand with his new woman. We locked eyes. I looked away fast. I didn't want him to think I still had feelings for him because it was pretty evident that he no longer had them for me and I believed as I'd said before, that he hadn't had them for me in months, maybe even years before we decided to officially end it. He was just too afraid to tell me.

"Excuse me, ma'am," a cute, petite woman said. "I was told to give you these."

She started handing me one red rose after another!

"What?!" I asked, shocked that someone was giving me roses and I didn't even know who this person was, but then again, it was obvious who it was. It was Devin, even though he was with another woman. For some reason, I wasn't surprised that he would do this.

"Wow, Liz! Looks like someone here didn't want you to feel left out!" Laurel said.

"Wait, ma'am, there's more," the petite woman told me.

Several more people walked up to me with baskets of roses and started putting them all into my arms!

"What the?! Holy!" I said, since I didn't wanna cuss. "What?! Oh, my God! What is going on here?!" I kept saying as I was being handed so many roses I could barely hold on to them. I knew I had at least fifty of them in my arms and they kept handing me more!

What the?!

I couldn't believe this!

But I no longer believed that this was Devin who sprung for this many roses for me, considering the fact that his new woman only had one rose in her hand, and they stood by and watched as I was being handed more and more roses as people had their phones up getting pictures and videos of all of this.

I was *not* expecting this!

"Damn, Liz! Did you meet someone here during intermission that we don't know about?" Marlon asked as he laughed.

"I didn't meet anyone here!" I honestly replied with total shock and amazement that I now had well over a hundred roses in my arms and it was hard for me to hold on to them all. I looked at the people who were handing me these roses. "*Who?* Who is giving me all of these roses?! I have to have at least a hundred of them here!"

"Two-hundred. That's what we were instructed to give you. Here comes the rest of them," the petite woman said with a smile.

"I need help carrying these, you guys" I said to Laurel and Marlon.

"No problem," they replied, and grabbed an armful of them each.

This was nuts!

Who just paid for me to have two-hundred red roses and he didn't even know me?

Again, I knew this couldn't be Devin, who I locked eyes with once again as he stood with his woman watching me receive this very unexpected gift, and he looked just as shocked as I did.

As I walked towards the exit of the arena, people complimented me on the roses while even more held up their phones getting pictures and videos. I walked right past Devin and didn't acknowledge him because I knew at this point it wasn't him. He'd never bought me this many roses in the five years we were together, so what made me think he just bought me two-hundred of them? Especially when he was here with another woman.

As I continued to walk towards the exit between Laurel and Marlon, I locked eyes with a gorgeous man sitting on an end seat. He was wearing a black suit, white collared shirt with no tie, and looked as if he had just gotten off of work before he came to the show, and most of all, he was all alone.

This was him.

I smiled as I walked up to him. "Hi."

"Hi," he replied with a smile.

This felt really awkward, but I knew he was the one who gave me these two-hundred roses, and I had to thank him for it. And I knew there was a reason why he gave them to me, but I was hoping it wasn't for the last reason it could've been for, but I was about to find out.

"Um, thank you. I wasn't expecting even one rose tonight, much less two-hundred of them."

He kept his smile as he stared at me and then stared at the roses. "They're beautiful."

"They are," I said with a smile.

This was *really, really* awkward.

"Um . . . ," I said, since I didn't know what else to say.

"Excuse me."

I turned around, as did Laurel and Marlon.

"Hi, I just wanna introduce myself. I'm Jeff Vick. I'm the one who gave you all of the roses."

He was not who I was expecting. He looked like he just came from the Consumer Electronics Show, and he was very nice looking. He had dark skin, a bald head, wore black frame glasses, and was wearing a plain white T-shirt with blue jeans, and was very clean-shaven and in great shape. He continued to smile at me as he stood with his hand extended out.

I felt very embarrassed. I tried to still hold on to all of these roses he gave me as I shook his hand. "Oh, my God. Wow." I lowered my head and felt like burying them in all of these roses. "I'm so embarrassed. I'm sorry. Thank you so much."

He smiled with a nod. "No problem at all, and you're welcome. I didn't get your name?"

"Liz. Liz Green," I replied with a smile.

"Nice to meet you, Liz Green," he replied as we shook hands again, and it was still very hard for me to since I had so many of these roses.

I introduced him to Laurel and Marlon.

"Well, thank you so much again for giving me these. It made this night a lot better," I said with a smile.

"Glad to hear it," he replied with a smile.

We all walked out to the parking lot.

"Where are you parked?" he asked.

"Right over there in the parking structure. I came here with my sister and her husband."

He nodded with a smile. "Well, I would like to get to know you more. Do you have time tonight for a late dinner?"

I looked at Laurel; she smiled big. "Um, sure."

"We'll take care of all of these beautiful roses for you, Liz. Go on," Laurel replied while still keeping that big smile, and she and Marlon took the rest of the roses from me.

Jeff and I continued to walk in the parking lot towards wherever his car was, and there was a big crowd standing around in the parking lot. He led me over to a beautiful red Ferrari. He opened the door for me and I got in while people stared at us.

Okay, I knew I was dreaming now.

We drove off to people getting pictures and videos on their phones.

"Well, I guess I don't have to ask how you're doing," I said.

He laughed as he kept his eyes on the road. "I do okay."

"Um, driving a Ferrari is doing a little better than okay, Jeff!"

He laughed again. "It is. I'm a retired doctor— neurosurgeon. And you?"

"A healthcare administrative coordinator that dreams of retiring at the age that you did and I don't even know how old you are."

"I'm 38," he replied with a smile.

"38? Wow! You must've known what you wanted to do from the start, huh?"

"Pretty much. I always dreamed of being a doctor, and I did get lucky to be able to retire early. I actually didn't think it was gonna happen this fast."

"But it's a good thing that it did, huh?"

"Yeah, it's always a good thing."

I looked down at my phone. It was a text from Laurel:

He drives a fuckin' Ferrari, Liz? DON'T BLOW THIS!!!!!!

I grinned as I shook my head. I didn't respond to her. I looked up and locked eyes with Jeff as we sat at a stoplight.

"So, how old are you?" he asked.

"32," I replied.

"I thought you were only in your early-to-mid 20s."

"Wow, thank you," I replied as I blushed. "Is it okay that I'm in my 30s?"

"Absolutely. I prefer it. I don't like extremely young women. They have a lot of growing up to do in my opinion. I rarely meet ones that are beyond their years in intelligence and with everything else."

"It's rare, but they're out there," I said with a smile.

"I forgot to ask, what's your favorite food?"

"Tacos," I replied.

We were coming up on a Taco Bell. He turned into the parking lot.

"Is this okay?" he asked with a smile.

"It's fine," I replied, even though I had it for lunch at work yesterday. But I was in no position to complain about a man taking me to Taco Bell who gave me two-hundred red roses at a concert that I wasn't sure whether or not I wanted to attend, and now I was riding in his beautiful red Ferrari on our way to a late-evening dinner. I couldn't even make any of this up.

Several minutes later, we had our food and were the only ones sitting in the dining area. We had a perfect view of his car, and I didn't blame him for not wanting to have it out of his sight.

Four men stood outside of a black Cadillac Escalade as they ate their food and stood right next to his car.

"Jeff, those guys are standing pretty close to your car," I said, and then ate some more of my nachos.

"It's cool. They're my friends. They're just looking out for my car, that's all."

"Oh," I replied with a smile. "So, they followed us here?"

"Yeah, they did. I hope you don't mind."

"Not at all," I replied with a smile. "Um, should I consider this a date?"

"If you want," he said with a smile. "We just met, and I was getting hungry since I hadn't eaten in hours. I didn't think I would see a woman like you at the show tonight."

I found this interesting. "A woman like *me*? What do you mean?"

"First of all, a woman fully dressed. I honestly don't know why some women feel that they have to walk out of the house half-naked to impress a man, and especially if they're with one. I'm one who's not impressed. Just wanted you to know that."

I laughed. "Yeah, there were some women who needed to put a lot more on than what they walked out of the house with on; it's like that at every show I go to. I just don't feel the need to dress like that, never have and never will. I feel that it's negative attention. You are what you attract."

"You got that right, Liz. When I saw you, I said, 'Wow, she's beautiful. She can't be single.'"

I blushed. "Thank you. And I am single." I took a sip of my Mountain Dew.

"I like women who have respect for themselves, and to me, it all starts with how you represent yourself when you go out in public. I don't mind dresses or skirts, but some of what I saw tonight was beyond ridiculous. You completely stood out to me with your sexy white short-sleeve shirt on, cropped jeans, and your black Valentino Rockstud shoes. We look like we came there together."

"Yeah, we did," I said with a smile. "And you know your shoes. And I couldn't help but notice your $2,020 Louis Vuitton Creeper boots. Those are dope. I instantly recognize them since the president of the company I work for wore the exact same pair on our casual day we have three times a month."

"Is he black?" he asked with a grin.

"Asian," I replied.

He nodded with a smile. "Yeah, I'm pretty basic when it comes to clothes, but I do love shoes. It's the one thing I admit to spending a lot of money on."

"But money doesn't seem like an object since you drive a Ferrari."

He grinned. "Not anymore," he replied, and took a sip of his Baja Blast drink. "But, Liz, I felt instantly connected to you. I'm sorry if I blindsided you with all of those roses. I couldn't take my eyes off of you every time I saw you there. I asked how many did they have left back there and they told me they could get me as many as I wanted. I wanted you to have more than what I saw other women getting from their men because it didn't look like you were having a good time."

"I wasn't," I admitted. "But you made it one of the best nights of my life when I was surprised with those roses from you. I initially thought they were from my ex because he was there, but he was there with another woman and has never, ever given me that many roses in the five years we were together. And then I thought it was the man in the suit until you stopped me from embarrassing myself more than what I was doing and told me it was you."

"You seemed surprised," he said with a grin.

"I was, I'm not gonna lie."

He nodded with a smile. "I know women look at me and think I'm a classic nerd; an old-school nerd. And most women don't like nerds."

I laughed. "Well, contrary to what they think, I love nerds; old-school nerds. I don't like thugs or any men who try to be and/or think they're one. Never been my type and never will be. If women act like they want men like that so bad and wanna pass over good men like you, well, let them. They don't deserve you."

"Thank you, Liz. And I feel that most men don't deserve you."

I felt we were really connecting. I was now forgetting all about my ex and him being with another woman tonight. Things don't work out for a reason, and now I was seeing firsthand that this was quite possibly true. I wanted to take things slow with Jeff, and I was hoping he would wanna do the same with me.

"It must've hurt for you to see your ex with another woman at the show tonight especially since it hasn't even been a year since the two of you ended your relationship, huh?" he asked, and then ate some more of his food.

"More than I wanted to admit, but I have to admit that I almost forgot all about him when I was being handed those roses. I did think it was him that paid for them at first, but the amount I was getting handed quickly changed my mind. I feel like this was a sign with you doing this that it's definitely time for me to move on."

He nodded. "I'm glad I was able to help it along. I haven't been in a serious relationship in years. Too many years to count. I've just had a problem with women only wanting to be with me more for the wrong reasons rather than for the right ones."

"And I can see how that can happen. You're obviously very wealthy. I'm sure you have women wanting to be with you all the time."

"But that's just it. They wanna be with me all of the time for the wrong reasons rather than for the right ones, and I'm tired of it. I wanna settle down, but I wanna settle down with the right woman. I've never been married and don't have any children. What about you?"

"Same here," I honestly replied. "I said I was not having kids unless I was married, and I meant it and still mean it. My sister got pregnant with her first and only child so far three years *after* she was married. We come from a two-parent household from parents who were married before they had the two of us like the way it should be and always be."

"We come from the same family structure. I always said I would never disappoint them and have kids out of wedlock, especially now. They're waiting for me to find a woman that loves me for who I am and wants me to marry her when I do."

"She's out there, Jeff."

He smiled as he kept staring at me. "She sure is."

I turned on the lights to my bedroom and found Laurel sitting in a chair by my desk. My roses were put in several vases and were evenly displayed throughout my room. It looked like a flower shop. "How did I know you were gonna wait up for me?"

"You knew I was going to!" she laughed. "The rest of your roses are in vases all over this house. I thought they were too pretty to just have in your room."

"Thanks a lot!" I laughed. I put my bag on my purse hook. "So, what is it that you wanna know? And if you think I slept with him I didn't, okay? Especially not on a first date."

"So it was a first date?"

"Yeah, we said we might as well call it that since we were both hungry for a late dinner."

"And where did he take you?"

"Taco Bell."

"Taco Bell?!" she said as she frowned with disappointment. She laughed. "Liz, are you for real? He took you to *Taco Bell*?! I know it's one of your favorite fast-food restaurants, but I thought he would take you somewhere a little more upscale."

"Well, he asked me what my favorite food was, and I said tacos. We were approaching Taco Bell and he turned into it. Hey, who was I to complain about where he took me for a date that I was not expecting to go out on with a guy I met at a concert I really didn't wanna go to, and who gave me two-hundred red roses at the end of it?"

"And who drives a Ferrari, don't forget that!"

"How can anyone forget that!"

We laughed.

"So, what does he do for a living?"

"He's a retired doctor; neurosurgeon."

"Damn, he must've been one of the best in the business since he drives a car like that!"

"Yeah, he must've been. I think he's also just from a superrich family as well. Maybe he didn't have to work after all."

"Well, whatever it is that he does, Liz, here's your chance to be in another relationship, a serious one. I know it hasn't been even a year since you and Devin broke up, but things like this happen for a reason."

"I just wanna take things slow with Jeff. I felt like everything was moving so fast tonight. I still feel like I'm dreaming."

"Did he take you back to his house?"

"Not at all. We went from Taco Bell right to here. I told him I was tired and just wanted to get some sleep. He said he'll call or text me later on today."

"I know you're looking forward to it!"

I nodded. "Yeah, but like I said, I don't know how all of this is gonna turn out. I felt like we really connected once we talked, but you just never know. I just don't know if I'm ready to start a relationship with someone again this fast. It feels like yesterday that Devin and I mutually ended our relationship, and you see how he was there tonight with another woman."

"And that's all the more reason why you need to officially move on, Liz. Jeff is a sign that you need to; I really believe that. I don't think he gave you all of these roses because he was just showing off how much money he has. He didn't even know you. It was obviously something about you that he felt a true connection with."

"Or he just felt sorry for me because I looked so pitiful throughout the show."

"Stop it, Liz, okay? Stop. I don't think you realize already just how lucky you got with him. He's a nice-looking man, he's obviously got money, and he's very interested in you. He could've given any single woman there tonight all of those roses, but he gave them to you and you were trending on social media because of it. Even the arena's social media pages have pictures and a video of it, saying that you were a very lucky woman to receive all of those roses."

I smiled. "Send all of those to me because I wanna tell him and send them to him."

"I will."

"And that's just it. I don't wanna blow anything with him. This is clearly a man who can have just about any woman he wants, and he showed an interest in me. I'm really flattered."

"Well, you obviously have what he's looking for, Liz, so like I said, this is officially your chance to move on, so as I said again, ***don't blow it***! Good night."

I laughed. "Good night."

I stared at all of the beautiful roses around my room that she put in these vases. I couldn't believe that I left here with nothing but my bag and at the end of the show ended up with two-hundred roses from a very wealthy man *and* went out on a date with him tonight. I believed that Jeff could really get any woman he wanted, and he chose to have an interest in me. And I was gonna do all I could to keep his interest in me because the last thing I wanted to do was blow a chance of being with someone that I didn't even know existed until I was given a bunch of roses that I wasn't expecting to get. I believed that things did happen for a reason, and what happened tonight was proof of it.

CHAPTER TWO

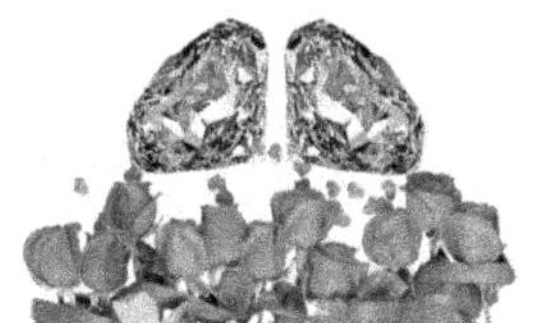

"LIZ!" Laurel shouted.

I jolted upright out of a deep sleep. "What? What is it?"

"You gotta come downstairs right now! Something's going on!"

I jumped out of bed and ran downstairs with her. She quickly led me to the front window. "What the hell?!"

There were reporters everywhere at the end of our driveway!

"What are they doing? What the hell are they here for?" I asked.

"They were asking for you, Liz," she replied. "I told them that you were sleeping and that I would have to see if it was okay that you wanted to talk to them."

"Talk to them about what?" I asked, as we still stood discreetly looking out of the front window while my hair was matted all over my head. "I can't go out there looking like this! And I'm not going out there until I find out what they wanna talk to me about!" I said in a panic.

"Calm down, Liz. Go and fix yourself up and then go out there," Laurel said.

Marlon came up to the window with his coffee mug. "Looks like you're already a celeb, Liz!"

"Celeb? What the hell would I be a celeb for? What is all of this about?" I walked away from the window and paced back and forth. "Um, could the two of you tell them I would be ready to talk to them in about twenty minutes?"

"Sure, sis," she replied.

"Okay, here we go," I said, almost a half hour later, and opened the front door and stepped out as Laurel and Marlon stepped out behind me. A rush of cameramen and reporters came to the front porch with their microphones and cell phones sticking all in my face.

"Liz Green, how was your date with the billionaire Jeff Vick last night?" a reporter from a black media channel asked.

"What?!" I asked, shocked that she'd asked this. And it was because she said the word that I was never expecting to hear when it came to me going out on a date with someone, anyone—billionaire.

Billionaire.

"No, you're mistaken. Jeff is not a billionaire. He would've told me that last night," I replied.

"I knew it!" Laurel said with a big smile.

The media laughed as they nodded in agreement.

"Well, it's confirmed that he is only one of two black billionaires in his age range in this world," another reporter said.

I was very well aware of who the other one was besides Jeff, but if Jeff was really a billionaire then like I'd told them, he would've personally told me last night. "He would've told me," I said again. "Why would he leave a big piece of information like that out about himself?"

"We don't know, Liz, but it's been confirmed. Here's my phone for proof," a reporter said, and then handed me her phone.

I took the phone from the reporter and saw proof myself that I officially had a date with a real-life billionaire, and a black one at that. Jeff was listed with a net worth of $2.9 billion. I *still* couldn't believe he didn't tell me anything about it last night.

"Are you looking forward to more dates with Jeff Vick, Liz?" another reporter asked.

"She most definitely is!" Laurel replied with a big smile.

Marlon and the media laughed.

"Excuse me, I need to get back inside. Have a nice day, everyone," I said, and walked back inside the house. Marlon and Laurel followed me.

I poured myself a cup of coffee and then sat at the kitchen table where they joined me. "I don't know what to think of all of this, guys."

"Liz, I don't see how you can think that any of this is bad. This is the best thing that can happen to a woman," Laurel said.

"I agree and I'm not even a woman," Marlon said.

Laurel laughed as she nodded in agreement.

I smiled, and then sighed. "I just don't understand why he didn't wanna tell me this last night. He knows that he's a billionaire and he left it out. I think it's a big deal to be a billionaire because there are very few of them in this world, and even fewer black ones."

"You can say that again," Laurel replied, and then sipped some more of her coffee. "I was a little tired myself last night, and especially after I put all of those roses in the vases for you and put them all over this house. That's why I forgot to look him up myself to see what was up with him. He just didn't look like an athlete or any type of entertainer, you know? I knew it was something bigger about him."

"But I know he didn't become a billionaire by being a neurosurgeon. They make a ton of money but unfortunately not billions," I said.

"Yeah, unfortunately not," Marlon replied.

"If he calls or texts me, I'll ask him."

"Wait, what do you mean *if*?" Laurel asked.

I shrugged. "Well, he said that he would, but I don't know that for sure. You know, I don't even know if he was being sincere about there not being another woman in his life, especially now since I found out that he is a billionaire. A man like him has got to have some side chicks somewhere."

"Take it from a man, Liz. I hate to say this to you, but he probably does," Marlon informed me.

Laurel shook her head. "Yeah, well, if he does then she or they don't mean anything to him. There's a difference between a side chick and a woman he wants a serious relationship with, and it seems to me he's looking for someone that he wants a serious relationship with."

I looked at her. "You think so?"

"Yeah, Liz, I do. I don't think he would've given you two-hundred roses and took you to Taco Bell last night if he wasn't serious about getting to know you," she said.

Marlon almost spit out his coffee! "Sorry, Liz. That just sounds funny every time I hear it since your sister told me earlier. A billionaire took you to Taco Bell after giving you two-hundred roses!"

I grinned. "Well, maybe he didn't want me to get used to eating at fancy restaurants all of the time. After all, we didn't know that we were gonna end up going to a late dinner last night. We didn't even know each other before the concert started."

"But it's clear that he wants to get to know you," Laurel said.

"Yeah, that's what he told me."

"And he could've bought all the women in that arena that many roses last night, whether they were single or not," Marlon said.

"And I would've accepted them!" Laurel said.

"Over my dead body!" Marlon said.

We all laughed.

"But seriously, guys. I don't know how to handle all of this. Being a billionaire is equated to being a celebrity, and now anyone that is perceived to be dating one is all of the sudden thrusted into a spotlight that they're not ready for or used to, at least I'm not."

"Liz, you'll do just fine. You got us," Laurel assured me. "We're not gonna let the pesky media ruin a potential relationship that you can have with Jeff. Maybe he hasn't been with anyone serious or is not with anyone serious since the media all came here, so maybe he's already serious about you, Liz."

I sighed. "Well, he did tell me that he hadn't been in a serious relationship in years, so now since this all happened with the media showing up here, I believe him."

"I believe him, too," she said.

"And take it from a man, I believe him as well," Marlon said.

CHAPTER THREE

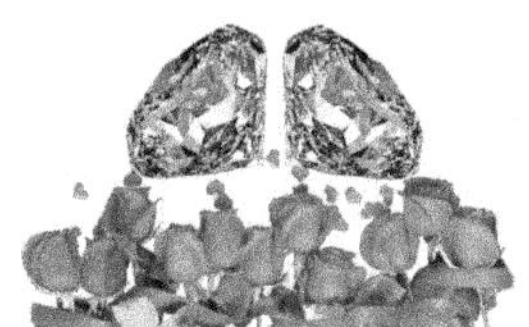

Up for a little shoe shopping?
Jeff.

He texted me. I didn't know what I was thinking; I just didn't know if he would. I mean, it was not like I had sex with him on our first date because even if he wanted to as my way of thanking him for giving me all of those roses last night, it was not gonna happen no matter what.

I texted him back:

Sure.

Great. I'll come get you in a few hours.

Sounds good.

But this wasn't good for me since I was broke and wasn't gonna get paid until next week. I wanted to beg Laurel or Marlon for a loan but then they would've looked at me like I was nuts since they knew who I was just out on a date with last night, and it was the same person I was going shoe shopping with.

"So, how was your morning?" Jeff asked me as he drove us in his brand-new Bugatti to one of the many upscale malls.

"Interesting," I replied with a smile.

"I'm sorry about that."

I looked at him. "Sorry about what?"

"Sorry about all of that media showing up at your house this morning. My sister texted it to me. I actually watched the video of them asking you all of those questions about me being a billionaire and everything. Sorry I didn't tell you."

"How come you didn't tell me?" I asked since I really wanted to know.

He shrugged as he kept his eyes on the road. "I didn't think it was that important."

"It wasn't important?" I asked, shocked that he'd said this. "Are you serious, Jeff? You don't think being a billionaire is important, and especially being a *black* billionaire isn't important?"

He grinned. "Well, if you put it that way, Liz, yeah, it's important, especially to our people."

"It most certainly is!" I said. "Sorry, I don't mean to sound so serious and all, but it is serious, Jeff. You're the one percent of the one percent. There's only one other black man like you in your age range in this whole world. That's something that should not be deemed as unimportant."

"I guess I'm just still shocked, that's all. I didn't grow up rich, but I did grow up in a middle-class family that took education and the importance of money seriously. I guess you can say that I've been an educated lame since birth."

"There's nothing lame about being educated."

He smiled. "You're right, Liz, it's not. I never thought it was."

"We need more men like you, like, seriously."

"And we need more women like you."

I blushed. "Thanks, Jeff."

We stared at each other at a stoplight.

I felt like I was in a dream. Here I was going out with confirmed billionaire Jeff Vick to a fancy, upscale mall to do some shoe shopping, and each time we talked like this, I felt that we were connecting more and more.

Several minutes later we were at the store, and it already felt different to me walking in here with someone who could literally buy anything they wanted in here, and I felt it was an honor to witness a billionaire shop. What was even more interesting was witnessing how he would be treated by these sales associates because a lot of them were not welcoming to us as well as to others—just to be fair—but especially to us, so I was very curious to see how this experience would go.

We walked directly over to the women's shoe department.

I looked confused. "What are we doing over here?"

"Ladies first," he replied with a smile.

I couldn't believe this was happening. But it didn't take but only a few seconds for my eyes to be completely drawn to a beautiful pair of Jimmy Choo Romy 85 shoes that were covered in beautiful red sparkling crystals. The ultimate ruby slippers. I'd seen these online several times, but it was nothing like seeing them in person. I picked up the shoe and flipped it over.

$2,850.

I put the shoe back in its rightful place.

"Those are beautiful," Jeff said with a smile.

"Yeah, they are," I replied. "But way too expensive."

"It's on me if you want them," he said.

I gave him a shocked look that I couldn't hide if my life depended on it. He was willing to buy me a pair of *$2,850* shoes that I had no idea in the world where I would wear them to. "Um, thanks for the offer. But I have no idea where I would wear them. I have nothing formal coming up."

"I got the perfect place you can wear them to."

I looked confused. "Okay. Where?"

"To my parents 40th wedding anniversary. It's tomorrow night. I hate to tell you on such short notice, but I'd love for you to be my date."

I was flattered. "Yes, I'd love to."

A sales associate walked up to us. "Hello, Jeff. How are you?"

"Hey, Anne. I'm just fine. This is my friend, Liz."

She extended her hand out for a shake. "Nice to meet you, Liz."

"Nice to meet you as well," I said with a smile as we shook hands.

She looked at the shoe. "Those are absolutely stunning, aren't they?"

"Yeah, even more beautiful in person," I replied with a smile.

"What size do you need?" she asked, as if she just knew he was gonna buy them for me.

"A 39," I replied.

"Be right back," she said as she walked away with the shoe in her hand.

I couldn't believe this was happening. If they had my size, he was gonna buy them for me. I'd never had a pair of shoes this expensive before, not even close.

Minutes later, I was trying on the most expensive pair of shoes to ever be on my feet. They were absolutely stunning. I turned myself around in the mirror several times as I stared down at them in total admiration and was glad that the heels on them were just the right height so I could walk perfectly in them. I *still* could not believe that he was gonna buy them for me until they were actually bought.

Jeff smiled as he nodded in approval. "Beautiful. It's something about a woman wearing a pair of beautiful, sparkling shoes."

"It makes us feel like queens, at least it does to me!"

"And you look like a queen wearing them," he said with a smile.

I blushed. "Thank you, Jeff." I began walking around the area as I turned it into my own catwalk. Women in this area stopped and stared and told me how beautiful these shoes looked on me and ask me was I buying them. I told them that Jeff was buying them for me; they told me I was one lucky woman. I couldn't agree enough.

As I walked around now inadvertently showing off, my right foot got caught in a woman's purse strap and I fell forward towards Jeff, and we both fell to the ground with me on top of him!

"JEFF! LIZ!" a man shouted.

We looked in this man's direction and right into the lens of his camera!

The flash almost blinded me.

. . .

Laurel was now parading around in my shoes. "Wow, Liz. These are absolutely beautiful. Thank goodness we wear the same size. Looks like you got a real keeper here," she said, as she admired my shoes on her feet in my mirror.

"We're just friends. He even said so. He told the sales associate that sold us the shoes that we were friends when he introduced the two of us. She knew him by name. He told me later that she usually works over in the men's shoe department but she was working there today. She gave me her card as well," I said with a smile.

"Yeah, I'm sure Jeff does a lot of business there."

"He does. Shoes are his thing."

She looked at me. "And I hope you didn't have to do anything to get these from him, Liz."

"No, Laurel, I didn't. I'm serious. He offered to buy them for me so I let him. I even initially turned them down because I told him I had nothing formal coming up to wear them to, and he said he wanted me to be his date to his parents 40th wedding anniversary, so I accepted."

She smiled. "Looks like the two of you are getting serious already."

"I just wanna take things slow with him. I've never been with a billionaire before. I still don't know if there's other women out there that he could be seeing." I sighed. "Laurel, I'm so nervous about meeting his parents, and this soon at that. I don't know if they're gonna like me even though I'm only his friend."

"Are you sure about that?" Marlon said as he walked into the room with his phone in his hand as he grinned big. "Looks like someone got you and Jeff in a pretty naughty position!"

I took his phone from him. I sighed as I shook my head. "I knew that dude was gonna put that picture up of us. I knew he was up to no good because I figured he was following us; I didn't say anything to Jeff."

"Who is he?" Marlon asked.

"Beats the hell out of me," I replied. "Probably just some dude taking pictures of billionaires or something, and especially when they're with women, obviously. Look, guys, it's not how it looks on there. I was walking around with the shoes on and ended up getting one of the heels of the shoe caught in a woman's purse strap since her purse was sitting on the floor, and I fell towards Jeff which made him lose his balance and fall to the ground and I landed on top of him, and the dude called both of our names and quickly took the picture when he saw both of us looking at him. That's the real story."

Laurel nodded with a smile. "We believe you."

"Me too," Marlon replied.

"And, Liz has another date with him tomorrow," Laurel informed him with a big smile. "And I need to see what's in that garment bag because I know it's a dress."

"Yes, it's a dress," I confirmed. I took it off the hook on my closet door and unzipped it. I pulled it out to Laurel's gasping and Marlon nodding in approval.

"Wow, Liz. This looks expensive as hell! She looked at the designer. "*Oscar de la Renta*? Yeah, this is very expensive!" She flipped over the price tag. "*$5,990*?! Damn! You're gonna be the belle of the ball tomorrow night, aren't you?"

"I don't know about that," I honestly replied. "Given that he's a billionaire that pretty much makes his whole family billionaires as well, so I know I'm gonna be in the house with some pretty fancy people and the women are gonna be wearing dresses that cost this much, so I'll just be another woman there."

"But you'll be there with the billionaire son of the parents celebrating their anniversary. That's not something every woman can say," Laurel said.

"Jeff just wants me to fit in, that's why he bought these things for me."

"Is that what he said?" she asked.

"No, but I know that's what he was thinking," I replied.

"And now I *really hope* you're telling the truth about not having to do anything for him to have bought you a pair of *$2,850* shoes and a *$5,990* dress," she stressed as she gave me a serious look.

Marlon looked up at me from his phone with a grin.

"I'm only gonna say this one more time. I didn't have to give Jeff anything for him to have given me these nice things. He can afford it. It's nothing to him but it's a very big deal to me. We're friends. I greatly appreciate it and take nothing at all for granted."

"And this is why people have a right to take that photo seriously of the two of you already," she said.

But I didn't know how serious Laurel and everyone else should've taken it. We ended up in that position accidentally, but I knew how people would take it. But Jeff and I knew that we were just friends right now, and I was looking forward to this next date with him.

CHAPTER FOUR

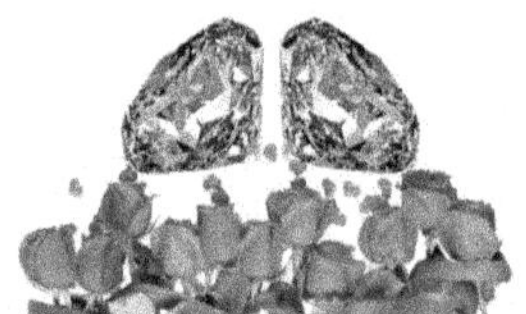

All eyes were on Jeff and me as we walked through the front doors of his parents' beautiful home, a home that they'd built and was a gift from Jeff to them. And it was truly a dream home with over 10,000 square feet of pure luxury, everything was top notch and looked like a home of a billionaire family. I was scared to walk on the beautiful white marble floors, and stared in amazement at the gorgeous wide double staircase with the most beautiful black wrought iron I'd ever seen as well as the most beautiful, huge chandelier hanging from the ceiling that literally looked like diamonds sparkling down on us. Everything from what I could see so far was absolutely exquisite. I knew this was a family with the utmost elegance and class as well as a legit billionaire family, so I knew I had a great friend already and was honored that he chose me to be his date for a milestone event in his family's history.

"Welcome to my parents' home," he said with a smile as he held my hand.

"Thank you. It's just downright gorgeous. Do I need to take off my shoes?" I asked.

"Not at all. Do you see anyone in here with their shoes off?" he asked with a smile.

I looked around. No one was barefooted. "No, everyone still has their shoes on."

"Let's go find my parents," he said with a smile as he held my hand and led me through the foyer.

I smiled as all eyes seemed to have been on us. It was as if people were waiting to see who he would show up with tonight, and I couldn't tell by anyone's expressions if they thought he made the right choice in picking me or not. But I kept a smile throughout it all because I loved my Oscar de la Renta Fil Coupé cocktail dress in a beautiful botanical print in black multicolor and I felt beautiful in it, something that I needed to feel since I'd never worn a dress as expensive as this.

Never.

I looked down at my beautiful red sparkling Jimmy Choo's on my feet. I felt like a queen.

Jeff kept sneaking peaks of me as we still walked through the house holding hands as he searched for his parents. "I know I told you this when I first saw you, but you look absolutely beautiful. You sure know how to put a look together and wear the hell out of it."

I blushed. "Thanks, Jeff. You look gorgeous yourself". And he absolutely did in his black Brioni tuxedo suit with a white shirt on but no tie. "But I meant to ask you, how come you're not wearing a tie?"

"I don't care for them," he said with a smile, and winked at me through his glasses. "My parents said they didn't mind as long as I wore a suit."

And he was probably one of the very few men out there that looked gorgeous in a suit like what he had on and was wearing the same glasses he was wearing when we'd met for the first time.

"JEFFREY VICK! It's about time you got here!" a beautiful woman said who wore a very unique bright yellow strapless mini dress covered in feathers, and I thought it was adorable.

"Hey, sis," Jeff replied with a smile.

They hugged and kissed each other on the cheek.

"Jenelle, this is Liz Green, my date for tonight," he said with a smile.

"Nice to meet you, Liz," Jenelle said with a big smile as she shook my hand. "You're really beautiful."

"Wow, thank you, Jenelle. So are you," I replied with a smile, and I'd meant it. She was really beautiful with her hair in black braids pulled up in a huge, super neat bun on the top of her head. Her makeup was beautifully put on and her slim, toned body clearly showed that she took very good care of herself just like her brother. I knew she could get as many men as Jeff could get women, and I knew the two of them were highly desirable especially since they were from a billionaire family.

"Thank you," she replied with a smile as she kept staring at me. "It's nice to meet the beautiful lucky lady who my brother sprung two-hundred roses for at that concert."

"I'm still shocked over it," I honestly replied. "I never saw it coming."

"That's my bro for you!" she said with a smile. "Well, let me get back to everyone. Oh, and just in case it doesn't work out between the two of you, you can still keep it in the family because now you know you have another option."

I gasped in shock! I didn't know what to say!

"Shut your Big Bird ass up and get out of here!" Jeff said with a laugh.

I laughed as well because I knew he was referring to her dress. "I love your dress."

"Thanks, babe. It's Attico, and I have them in all the colors they made of them," she replied with a smile. "At over $4,000 for each one, I couldn't help but get them all."

Over $4,000 *for each one*. Must be nice.

"Yeah, I see where the money I give you goes to," Jeff said with a grin.

"Hey, a woman has to look like a diva every day. Right, Liz?"

"Absolutely right," I replied with a smile.

"Where's Mom and Dad?" Jeff asked her with a grin.

"Somewhere in here," she replied as she kept smiling at me. "Well, let me go for real. I meant what I said, Liz."

"GO!" Jeff ordered with a laugh.

Jenelle laughed as she sashayed off from us.

I watched her as I smiled as people smiled and stared at her. "Wow, she's really beautiful. Is she serious? You know?"

"Yeah, she's serious. There's not a man in this world she wants. She's never been in the closet. Her girlfriend is around here somewhere so I was hoping she would see her flirting with you."

I laughed nervously. "Well, it did catch me off guard. I would've never known she was gay. I know you don't know who could be gay so I'm not ignorant in that aspect, but she is stunning. I'm sure men are very disappointed all the time when they find out that she is gay, huh?"

"Yeah, they are. I said it's the one thing I don't have to worry about is her being serious about men, but I gotta be serious about her trying to take my girlfriends!"

We laughed as he still held on to my hand as we continued to walk through this beautiful house. We stopped along the way for Jeff to say hello to people, and he introduced me to them all as his friend and date. I really felt included in this exclusive environment, and I already felt like it was a world's away from the life that I was used to.

Finally, we reached his parents.

"Mom and Dad, this is my friend and date, Liz Green," Jeff said with a smile.

"Nice to meet you, Liz," his mom said with a smile as we shook hands.

"Nice to meet you, too," I replied with a genuine smile back.

"Nice to meet you, dear," his dad said as we shook hands.

"Nice to meet you as well, Mr. Vick," I replied with a genuine smile at him as well. His parents were very nice people and I could see where Jeff and Jenelle got it from.

"We were wondering when we were going to meet the young lady who my son gave two-hundred roses to," his mom said with a smile. She looked at his dad. "You've never bought me that many roses in the forty years we've been married."

I gasped as I still tried to smile.

"Mom," Jeff said with a grin.

"That's a lie," his dad replied with a grin. "It may not have been two-hundred roses all at once, but you've gotten that many so don't stand there and tell stories."

We all laughed.

"Well, anyway, you see where Jeff gets it from," his mom said to me with a smile.

"Yeah, he gets it from me," his dad said with a laugh.

Once again we all laughed, and I felt very comfortable around them. It was like a relief because I knew I was going to meet them today.

"Excuse us," Jeff said, and held on to my hand once again.

"You're not leaving, baby, are you?" his mom asked.

"No, Mom, we're not. I just wanna mingle with some of the other guests and introduce Liz to some more people."

"Sounds good," his mom said with a smile.

We walked away from them still holding hands.

"Your parents are very nice and so down-to-earth," I said with a smile.

"Thank you. But how did you think they were gonna be?"

"I don't know," I honestly said. "I was so nervous I just didn't know what to expect."

"We're like any other family," he informed me.

"Now I see that," I said with a smile. But what I also saw all around me was something I didn't want to mention to him, and I knew I wasn't seeing things. I seemed to have been getting so many dirty looks from women while I held hands with him as we walked around this beautiful house and while he introduced me to people. It made me wonder what was really going on. "Um, where's the bathroom?"

"Just go straight down that hall. It's the second door on the left," he replied.

"Thanks. I'll be right back." I walked away from him as I went to the bathroom hoping that someone wasn't in it. As I walked down the hall, I came up on a room where the door was halfway opened. I saw a group of women in it talking as they seemed to have been freshening themselves up like what I wanted to do.

I heard my name, and stopped dead in my tracks.

"So that's the girl he bought all of those roses for? Are you kidding me?" the light-skinned one said who had dark and thick naturally curly hair that fell a little bit past her shoulders. I immediately named her NaturallyCurlyHair.

"Yeah, that's obviously her. When I saw the picture of her at the show with all of those roses I thought she looked pretty basic, and in person she still looks basic," another caramel-skinned woman said while she checked herself out in her Chanel compact mirror while fingering through her long, dark lace-front wig, so I named her Lace-FrontWig.

"What is wrong with Jeff? He can have any woman he wants and he picks a woman who's practically bottom shelf?" another light-skinned woman said with short blonde hair that was shaved off to an inch on each side and spiked up and back in the middle, resembling a female mohawk. I named her ShortBlondeHair.

"Well, it's clear that he doesn't think she's bottom shelf," LaceFron-tWig said. "She's probably just gonna be his date for tonight anyway. He's gonna get what he wants from her tonight and he'll be on to the next woman tomorrow, everyone knows that."

"We sure do," NaturallyCurlyHair said. "And you know she's gonna have to give him some pussy since you know he bought her that dress and those shoes she's wearing!"

They all laughed as they nodded in agreement.

"And she knows damn well she fell on him in that store on purpose; trying to look for the perfect photo op so she could be trending with him on social media," ShortBlondeHair said.

"That goes without saying. She wants people to believe she's officially his girl now. Like I said, I know why he did this shit, but I'm not fazed by it," NaturallyCurlyHair said.

"Don't be," LaceFrontWig said.

I sighed as I tried to suppress the tears that were welling up in my eyes. These women had no idea that I'd heard everything they'd said. Not only were they just downright nasty in terms of what they thought about me and they didn't even know me, but I was even more shocked that they would speak about Jeff like the way they had as if they'd all dated him . . . and they probably had because I had to admit that all three of them looked like his type.

I started to feel differently about fitting into his world.

"Liz?"

I turned around and stared Jenelle right in the eye. "Hey."

"Hi. Is something wrong?" she asked.

"Nothing," I replied with a fake smile.

The three women walked out of the room as they *still* talked about me.

"If she thinks she's gonna have anything serious with Jeff then she's really dreaming!" NaturallyCurlyHair said.

"EXCUSE ME?" Jenelle shouted at them.

All three of them turned around and looked shocked to find Jenelle staring right back at them with me by her side.

"Jenelle! Hey!" NaturallyCurlyHair said.

"Don't start with that fake-ass shit, Karis," Jenelle warned. "You know I've *never* liked you."

LaceFrontWig and ShortBlondeHair looked at Karis; she was speechless.

"I think the three of you owe Liz here an apology," Jenelle said.

I couldn't believe it! Jenelle was serious!

"For what?" LaceFrontWig asked.

"For talking shit about her just because she's my brother's date tonight, that's 'For what?', Beverly! The three of you are the biggest shit talkers I've ever seen. I don't even know how y'all got in here."

"Your brother invited us," ShortBlondeHair informed her. "And we weren't gonna turn it down."

"Yeah, Chloe, I believe that, because all three of you are very good at not turning anything down when it comes to super high-value men," Jenelle said.

Whoa, I thought. I tried to keep a smile, but I wanted to laugh. It was clear to me that she didn't like any of them and seemed to of had a lot of tea on them as well.

"Liz is a very sweet person, so stop the shit-talking and all of that immature high-school girls shit that all three of you have been doing tonight at this party. Think I haven't noticed? This is my parents' house and their wedding anniversary. My brother was being overly nice for inviting all three of you."

Damn! I thought. She was really going in on them and I wasn't gonna stop her.

"Liz is who my brother chose for his date tonight. He really likes her and there's nothing the three of you can do about it. And, Karis, you might have had a chance to marry Jeff if you didn't have a baby by that basketball player who already has nine kids by nine different women. Ten times the charm? Don't think so, whore!"

Beverly and Chloe looked at Karis, but she was speechless once again.

Jeff walked up to all of us. "What's going on?"

"Nothing, bro. Liz and I were just about to find you," Jenelle said.

We all walked off from Karis, Beverly, and Chloe. I looked back at them, and if looks could kill . . . .

"Well, let me find my girlfriend. She's probably getting hit on by a bunch of men so I'm gonna need to intervene. Excuse me," Jenelle said.

"Jenelle?" I said.

"Yeah?" she replied with a smile.

"Thank you," I said.

"You're welcome. Anytime, beautiful, anytime," she replied, and went on her way.

Jeff looked down at me as we continued to walk through the house. "What was that about?"

I sighed as I tried to smile, but just couldn't. "I don't wanna talk about it."

He stopped where he was at. "What is it, Liz?"

I sighed once again. "I think I should leave."

"Let's go somewhere private and talk. I got the perfect place," he said. He slowly held on to my hand and led me through the house and out a back door.

CHAPTER FIVE

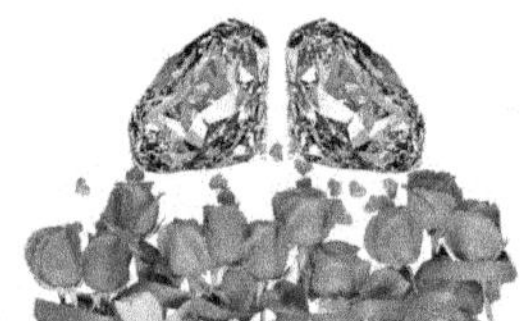

"It's a beautiful night," Jeff said, as we continued to hold hands as we walked through his parents' backyard to this mysterious perfect place. And this backyard was beautiful with a walking path and very well lit.

"It really is," I replied with a smile as I stared up at the beautiful sky and every star seemed as if it was shining tonight. "Where are you taking me?"

"You'll see," he replied with a smile.

I felt like we were walking for miles. We suddenly came up on a beautifully paved bridge that had beautiful black wrought iron fences and like the walkway, very well lit. As we walked across the bridge, I looked to my right and saw the most beautiful treehouse I'd ever seen. And it truly looked like a treehouse because it was high up in the trees, but this one was extraordinary. It was huge and had a huge pool that looked like it was hanging off of a cliff that sat right in front of it.

"Wow. A treehouse. And one of the biggest and most beautiful ones I've ever seen. Ever. This is truly a child's fantasy."

"And it was mine growing up, as well as my dad's. That's why I had this built for him." He opened the front door. "Come on in."

I walked into the most amazing and luxurious treehouse on the face of this earth, and I didn't think I was exaggerating. This was just downright beautiful; a true fantasy. It smelled of fresh wood, had the finest furniture, pictures of his family, and even vintage toys from his dad's childhood. "Your dad is a lucky man for you to have done something so amazing for him."

"He's responsible as to the reason why I'm a billionaire, and so is my mom. I had no problem fulfilling his childhood fantasy of wanting the best treehouse ever. I'm a treehouse lover myself, and had a very tiny one growing up. There was barely enough room for two people to fit into it, but my dad and I would talk in it when I just needed to get away from everything and everyone, and my sister and I would talk in it when we needed to get away from our parents. And, of course, I always took my friends to it as well since it was our secret hideaway, even though only two of us could barely fit in it at a time."

I laughed. "That's cute. But that's great that you're giving back to your parents for what they've done for you. I wish I could do the same."

"You can give back in more ways than you can imagine," he said with a smile. He went over to the refrigerator. "Do you want a drink?"

"No alcohol. I have a one drink limit at parties and other events, and since I had that while we were at the house, I'll just have a bottle of water."

"You got it," he said. He handed me a bottle.

"Thank you," I replied with a smile.

"Wanna sit outside since it's so nice?"

"Sure."

We sat down in the beautiful lounge chairs as we faced the pool.

"Never seen a treehouse with a pool," I said.

He laughed. "Yeah, I've come a long way since my little rickety treehouse when I was a child."

"Do you have one at your own house?"

He grinned. "Yeah, I do. Couldn't help it. But it's not rickety by any means."

"Oh, I bet it isn't!" I said with a smile.

He kept staring at me. "So, what's on your mind? How come you wanted to leave the party?"

I sighed. “I don’t wanna start anything.”

He sighed as he moved his chair closer to mine. He reached over and held both of my hands. “You’re not starting anything, Liz. Whatever you tell me I’m not gonna go back and tell my sister, parents, friends, no one. Okay?”

I nodded as we still held hands. I looked up at him as he stared back at me. “I don’t think I fit in with your lifestyle.”

“What?” he said in shock. “What brought this on all of the sudden? You seemed happy that you were here tonight up until I saw you in the hall with Jenelle. What happened?”

“I overheard those three women talking about me, Jeff. And they had nothing nice to say about me.”

He sighed as he shook his head. “Doesn’t surprise me. I knew I shouldn’t have listened to my friends and invited them. What did they say?”

“They said I was basic looking.”

“Bullshit. You’re far, far from it,” he replied, and took a sip of his drink. “What else?”

“That I was very close to being bottom shelf and that they didn’t know why you would give me two-hundred roses.”

“They’re just mad because I’ve never given any of them anything like that.”

I cracked a grin. “And that’s not all.”

“I bet.”

I sighed because I really didn’t know if I should’ve said this to him or not. “Um, one of them said that I was dreaming if I think I’m gonna have anything serious with you.”

“Which one said that?”

“Karis. And I only know her name because Jenelle said it.”

“That’s my ex-girlfriend,” he informed me. “The other two are her best friends, Beverly and Chloe. I can’t stand them. They’re always talking about people who they think has less than them; all three of them do, that’s why I’m not with Karis anymore, as well as the fact that she has a kid now by a basketball player. He doesn’t want anything to do with her and now she’s constantly calling, texting, emailing me about wanting a second chance, so yeah, I can see why her and her friends were talking about you. They're hating, Liz, that's the only reason why they were talking about you. They would've talked about any woman I walked in there with tonight."

I believed him. But this was *me*, and if I wanted to have a serious relationship with Jeff then it was clear that there was a lot I was gonna have to put up with, and jealous, hating-ass ex-girlfriends of his and her friends was pretty much a given. "Oh, and Karis also said that I fell on you on purpose in the store for a photo op so we could trend on social media."

"She's full of shit," he said. "And she needs to stop taking thirst-trap pictures of herself and posting them if she wants to talk about photo ops, but I digress. We both know the truth behind that picture of us."

"You don't have any feelings for her, do you?"

"Absolutely none, Liz. If I did then I would've showed up with her tonight. I couldn't take her nastiness anymore about everything. She's just a condescending bitch that thinks she's better than everyone else and always tried to claim to me that she was different than all of the other women out there, but she showed that she was no different from any other woman by having a baby by a man who has multiple children by multiple different women. She thought he was gonna feel differently about her and marry her and then wanted to rub it in my face, but her plan backfired and failed miserably. She does want me back, Liz, and even said so just even a few days ago, but I told her that I've moved on, and if showing up with you was not an indication of that then I don't know what to tell her."

Something about this made me feel uneasy. "You didn't give me all of those roses and wanted me to be your date tonight as well as bought me this dress and shoes I'm wearing just to make her mad, did you?"

"No, Liz, I didn't. Like I said to her, I've moved on, and you're proof that I did, but I don't want you to ever think that I did all of this to make her mad and jealous. I like you. I really wanna get to know you more. I'm just tired of all of the bullshit that goes on in my circle. I just wanna be with someone who is serious about being with me as I'm serious about being with her. Because of my status, it's hard for me to find a good woman, but I knew you were a good woman when I saw your true reaction about getting all of those roses; you weren't expecting them."

"Most women would've reacted like me."

"You'll be surprised, Liz. A lot of women think they're always entitled to stuff like that. I could tell that you weren't that type. I couldn't take my eyes off of you that night."

I blushed. "I felt so lonely there. The last thing in the world I was expecting was you giving me those roses. I can't believe that it's led to what it's already led to. I mean, don't get me wrong, I was having a great time tonight with meeting your parents, sister, friends and all, but when I overheard those women talking like that about me and they don't even know me, I felt like an outsider once again."

"And that will be the last time they'll make you feel that way," he promised.

But I couldn't be so sure.

He looked at his phone. "Excuse me. I need to use the bathroom."

"Okay," I replied with a smile. I suddenly thought about what he'd said. He had to go use the bathroom. This treehouse had a bathroom in it. Wow. And why not? It had a pool outside and this treehouse had to of been at least 2,000 square feet.

But I was nosey. I got up and walked back inside. I saw a door shut and the light on so this was obviously the bathroom he was in, but I heard him talking in it instead of using it.

"I'm sorry, okay . . . I can't talk right now . . . I'll make it up to you."

I walked away from the door. I couldn't believe what I'd just heard. I walked back outside and sat back down.

He came back outside minutes later. "Sorry about that. I didn't expect to take that long in there."

"Can you take me home now? It's getting late and I'm getting tired."

He looked at me as if I was lying. "Is there something wrong?"

"I just wanna go home."

CHAPTER SIX

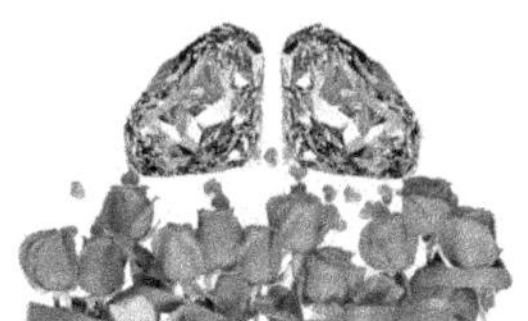

I stared at the dress I wore last night to the party as it sat in a chair in the corner of my room. My beautiful red sparkling shoes sat right below it. I sighed as I stayed in bed. I would've been up by now at least getting coffee since today was a Saturday and I didn't have to work today, but I just felt like pulling the covers back over me and rolling back over.

My door swung open.

"Aunt Lizzie!"

My beautiful niece. No matter what, she always made me smile. She was six years old and I felt already beyond her years in intelligence and maturity. She ran up to my bed in her soccer uniform since she had a game today.

"Hey, Autumn," I said as we hugged. "Ready for your big game today?"

"Not really," she honestly replied. "They're a tough team. They've only lost one game and we've only won one. I can't stand being on a losing team."

"Well, honey, it takes time to develop a good team. Everyone has to play their part in making a team better. But you all are not losers by any means."

"Yeah, I know. But I play my part better than anyone," she said. "No one just seems to put in the effort that I do. I feel like I'm out there running and kicking the ball by myself."

I laughed because I'd been to some of her games and it'd always looked that way. "Well, you're more advanced than the other players; more coordinated. You all are just kids, and you better thank God for that because you'll be an adult like me and your parents sooner than you know it."

"Yeah, Mommy and Daddy always say that to me," she said. "Are you coming to my game?"

"Not today. Rain check?"

"Of course," she said with a smile.

We hugged again.

She looked down at my shoes that Jeff bought me. "Oooooooh! These are *so pretty*!" she said in amazement as she held them up. "I love the color red! And they're so sparkly!"

I smiled as I nodded. "Thanks, baby. I love them, too. They were a gift."

"From your boyfriend?"

I grinned. "Well, yes. He's a boy and a friend."

"Mommy and Daddy says he's *really rich,*" she said with a big smile.

I laughed. "Yeah, he's really rich," I confirmed.

Laurel entered the room. "Autumn, come on, honey. You're gonna be late for your game. Your dad is already in the car."

"See you later, Aunt Lizzie!" she said.

"Good luck, baby," I replied with a smile. My smile disappeared from my face as soon as Autumn left out of the room.

Laurel stared down at me. "What happened last night?"

I shook my head. "I don't feel like talking about it. Go on, I don't wanna make y'all late for her game."

"Well, we'll talk about it later," she said as she still stared at me. "Bye."

"Bye," I replied, as I now sat on the side of my bed. I stared at all of the roses and they still looked as fresh as the day Jeff had given them to me. I didn't know what to think at this point about pursuing something serious with him. There were so many things I still didn't know and I felt I was still in the dark about, especially since I'd overheard him clearly talking to someone in the bathroom of his dad's treehouse, and it was clear he didn't want me to know who it was.

I toweled myself off after getting out of the shower when my phone lit up with a text.

Lunch?

It was Jeff.

I walked back into my room as I texted him back:

Sure. That's fine. I don't have any plans for today.

As I waited for him to text me back, I thought about asking him about the mysterious text that he'd obviously received last night that he didn't want me to know anything about. I already didn't like that he acted as if he had to go running off to the bathroom to talk to someone on the phone. I felt already that he was hiding something from me and I was determined to find out what it was.

Okay. I'll come get you in about an hour. And don't worry, I won't take you to Taco Bell.

I laughed as I texted him back:

That's nice to hear. Thanks.

"You're right, this is nothing like Taco Bell," I replied with a smile as I looked at my menu as Jeff and I sat in a private dining room at this expensive steak and seafood restaurant. The table was long enough to hold at least twenty people at it, so it felt awkward with just the two of us being in here with him sitting at the head of the table and me sitting to his left.

"I hope you don't mind that I wanted a little privacy so that's why I decided to get this room for us since no one had booked it," he said, and took a sip of his water.

"It's absolutely fine. It does look funny, though, that we're the only two in such a big room and there's enough seats at this table for at least ten or more people."

"It does look funny, but I just wanted to be able to talk to you and eat in peace without people staring at us and taking pictures and videos of us on their phone cameras."

"Thank you for respecting my privacy because I'm just not used to all of this."

He nodded as he stared at me as he put down his menu. "What was the real reason you wanted to leave last night?"

I sighed. Here was my chance to tell him. "I was just tired," I lied.

He grinned. "You didn't seem that tired all night."

I shook my head. "I just find it hard to fit into your world, that's all. I'll remember the night we met for the rest of my life, but it just seemed so different when just two days later, you bring me as your date to your parents anniversary party, and people looked at me as if I shouldn't have been there. Like I shouldn't have been wearing an expensive dress and expensive shoes, and your ex and her friends really thought I shouldn't have been because they knew for sure that you'd bought me those things, and what could I say? They were right because you did. It was the best gift I'd ever gotten from a man and I felt beautiful in what I was wearing, and they made me feel like shit."

"You did look beautiful in that dress and shoes, Liz, and I don't want you to ever feel like shit because of what some hating-ass women say. They're miserable. Karis is mad and jealous because she knows I will never take her back and have permanently moved on from her, and her friends are her friends and just like to talk shit about anyone who they think isn't on their level. That's why all three of them are single and probably will be for a long time because none of the guys I know in my circle wants to date them especially since they all have kids and have been married once before, except for Karis. These guys were even asking me did you have any friends that are single."

"Really?" I asked as I perked up. "Well, my sister is my best friend but as you know, she's married. My other friends are married, some are divorced, some have never been married but have kids and boyfriends and all. It's definitely slim pickings out there when it comes to someone with my status of being single, never married with no kids."

"You're the rarest of the rare, and I love it," he said with a smile. "Most men don't think women like you exist anymore, especially being in your 30s."

"We're definitely out here but hard to find, but you found me."

He nodded with a smile. "And I'm glad I did."

I felt better, but I still had questions. I was still curious about what I'd overheard him saying in the bathroom in his dad's treehouse. I didn't know whether or not I should've brought it up because I felt that he was still hiding something from me.

Minutes later, our food was brought to our table.

"Wow, that's the biggest lobster I've ever seen! I see why it cost $125," I said, as I stared at it in amazement.

"Yeah, it's big, and I'm eating every bit of it. This is what I usually always get when I come here since I think they have the best lobster," he replied, and poured hot butter on it.

I stared down at my Alaskan crab legs. I was almost afraid to eat them knowing that they were $65. "I'm glad they already have these cut open for me so I don't have to struggle cutting them open with a cracker and someone risking getting an eye injury from them flying everywhere if we were out in the main dining area."

He laughed. "Yeah, they make your eating experience a lot better here than at most places."

"And I have to say that I've never had crab legs for lunch," I said, and dipped half of the crab legs into its small cup of hot butter.

"This is one of the few times I had lobster for lunch. They actually don't serve it around this time, they just made an exception for us."

"Well, it's great to be you, huh? Money definitely talks, especially a billionaire's money."

"I hate to say it like this, but it does."

"Hey, it is what it is!"

We laughed as we continued to eat, and it was nice that we were in this private room so I could relax and we could eat in peace while enjoying our conversation.

We walked out of the private room and into the main dining area of the restaurant, and there sat Karis, Beverly, and Chloe! No one could pay them to smile at us.

"Hi, Jeff," they all managed to say.

"Ladies," Jeff said with a nod as he kept walking as we continued to hold hands.

I managed to crack a smile and was only doing it to be respectful because it was clear how they'd felt about me.

We weren't even past their table for a few seconds when they all erupted into laughter.

I didn't look back at them because I knew that was what they wanted me to do. I looked at Jeff. He kept walking as if he didn't hear them, but I know he did. It was pretty impossible not to since they were so loud. I felt at this point they were gonna do anything they could to destroy a potential serious relationship I could have with Jeff. They simply didn't think I belonged with him even though they didn't know a damn thing about me.

Minutes later, we were driving off from the restaurant.

I sighed. "Did you know they were gonna be there?"

"No, I didn't, Liz. I really didn't."

"Well, I don't think it's a coincidence that they were there the same time we were."

"I hate to agree with you, but I do. It's not like it's a hangout of theirs." He stared at me at a stoplight. "I'm sorry, Liz. I heard their laughing when we walked past their table; they were so damn loud I'm sure the people in the casino heard it. I'm gonna have to have a serious talk with them. I'm not gonna have this stalking shit."

"You think that's what they're doing already? I mean, we're not even boyfriend/girlfriend and they're already doing stuff like this?"

"Yeah, I think that's what they're doing. I'm not gonna lie to you, and like I said, I'm not gonna have this shit. I like you. I wouldn't have given you that many roses at the concert and took you out to a late dinner that night, bought you a beautiful dress and shoes, and brought you as my date to my parents anniversary party if I wasn't seriously interested in you. Karis just can't accept the fact that I've really moved on from her and I just can't say it enough, and her friends are just going along with it because all the three of them do is gossip, shop, and live on social media. I don't want a woman who's like that."

I smiled. He was serious. "Thank you, Jeff. That's what I needed to hear. And no, I'm not a social media freak. I only have one social media account and I'm hardly on it. It's just not my thing."

"Yeah, not mine, either. I like doing things in real life with people. I don't like to brag and show off and pretend that my life is something that it's not."

"But with you being a billionaire you really do live a fabulous life and you don't even have to try."

"And I want the right woman to share my life with, and Karis and millions of other women are not the ones."

But someone was the one, and I wasn't even sure if it was me. And I still didn't know who he was talking to that night when we were up in his dad's treehouse. This was gonna nag at me until I found out, but I didn't wanna seem nosey already. I looked at my phone. There was a text from my mom:

Hey, baby! How come you didn't tell me about your new billionaire boyfriend?! Call your Momma back as soon as you can!

I grinned. "It's my mom," I informed Jeff.

He smiled. "I'd love to meet her."

"And I know she'll love to meet you as well, otherwise she wouldn't have texted me. I know she saw all of the pictures of us on social media at your parents anniversary party, now she wants her turn in having us over her house so you can meet her and my dad. I know what she's doing."

"And I don't mind at all. Just let me know when."

I didn't know if this was even a good idea. I was still getting to know him and I wanted to take things slow. I already had three hating-ass bitches on my back, and one happened to be Jeff's ex-girlfriend, and I probably had many more out there that I didn't know about. I knew my mom, as well as my dad, wanted the best for me since my sister was married and we were their only children, and I was the only one that wasn't wifed up yet. But I didn't wanna get my mom, sister, dad, and especially my hopes up about Jeff, because little did anyone know, I was having second thoughts about all of this.

. . .

"Well, it's clear Jeff is still interested in you since he took you out for an expensive lunch this afternoon," Laurel said, as we sat in the kitchen and talked hours later.

I sighed. "Yeah, clearly he still is, and I'm still interested in him. But this is no ordinary relationship. He is a billionaire. On that alone he can get any woman he wants."

"And he clearly wants you," she replied, and sipped her early evening hot tea, as she always called it.

"Yes, I know, Laurel. But for how long is the question. I told you I just don't know whether or not I'm right for him. I have a right to have second thoughts about this because I'm not gonna be pushed around by some hating-ass bullying bitches who are just mad because he has no interest in them and has completely moved on from his ex. You know they were at the restaurant today when we were done eating in that private room? When we passed their table, they said hi to him first and he acknowledged them in return, but they said nothing to me. But as soon as we passed their table completely, they started laughing all loud like some stupid schoolgirls. They knew we were there, even Jeff knew. He said that restaurant is not a hangout of theirs."

"I know women like that can be hard to deal with, Liz, especially since one of them is his ex. But if you really like Jeff, you would do your best to ignore them because there're always gonna be women like them around, and I feel that you're doing a great job of that already, and I know Jeff notices that as well about you."

I smiled. "Yeah, he does."

"Good. And that ex of his clearly thinks that she's the one that should be with him and only him. I've seen her, I've seen all three of them and they think they're God's gift to men. It's clear that Jeff has an interest in you, Liz, *you*. I honestly don't think there's anyone else because he would not have been seen at all of these public places with you and this soon at that."

I shook my head. "I still don't know."

She sighed as she shook her head. "I just don't know what you're so unsure about, Liz. Right now, you are considered to be the luckiest woman in the world, especially being a black woman. Jeff is a billionaire, and a black one at that. It's clear that just his status alone he can get any woman he wants, *any woman*, and you know I mean regardless of color, and he chose you to have an interest in and it's clear he still has an interest in you. It's also clear that he's serious about you. I wouldn't blow this for the world, Liz, and especially not blow it because of some hating-ass bitches and second thoughts because of it. They would kill to be in your position and so would millions of other women. That ex of his had her chance with him and she blew it. Jeff having an interest in you is a chance of a lifetime for a woman, and I'm not just talking about black women, I'm talking about *all* women. But it's even more of a chance of a lifetime because you're black and he's a black billionaire."

I nodded with a smile. "When you put it in perspective it's a lot of think about, and everything seemed to have happened so fast. I am lucky that he has an interest in me, without a doubt. It's just that I have to get used to all of this, that's all."

"And that's perfectly all right. With real relationships, you have to take things slow, and there's no doubt that you will have second thoughts and doubts about things, it's only natural."

"And Jeff is no ordinary man. I've never been with a billionaire before, regardless of color. I'm having second thoughts because truth be told, Laurel, something bothered me about the night of that party."

Her interest was piqued. "What is it?"

I sighed. "While we were at his dad's treehouse—a *2,000* square-foot one at that—he looked at his phone and then excused himself to the bathroom. I was nosey, I'll admit, and went to the bathroom and listened outside the door. He was talking about how he was sorry to someone and that he would make it up to them."

Marlon walked into the kitchen.

"What was I supposed to think about what I'd heard?"

"That he has another woman," Marlon replied, and sat down at the table.

"Marlon!" Laurel said with disgust. "That's not necessarily true."

"The hell it's not," he replied with a slight grin.

I sighed. I believed him. "And this is exactly why I have second thoughts about pursuing a serious relationship with Jeff. He had a chance to tell me who it was yesterday *and* today, but he didn't tell me."

"I hate to say this, Liz, but it's none of your business."

"Marlon!" Laurel said. "Get out of here! I'm trying to have a conversation with her! You're just making her upset."

"I'm telling her the truth, Laurel," he replied. "Like I said, I hate to say this, but he would not have got up and left and went to the bathroom if it *wasn't* a woman he was talking to. Take it from a man, I know."

Laurel stared him down. "*You know*? Is there something you're not telling *me*?!" she said as her voice got louder.

"I didn't mean to start anything here," I said, because I didn't want the two of them getting into a fight.

"C'mon, baby. Don't be silly. It's just that as a man I know how other men are. I'm not hiding anything from you so don't even start that shit," he said, and then took a sip of his Hint cherry bottled water.

"Well, do you think I should still have Mom and Dad meet him since she invited him to dinner?" I asked.

"Of course, Liz. That's a given. How many chances are they gonna have a black billionaire over for dinner? And one that is interested in one of their daughters?" she asked.

"I agree with Laurel, Liz. This is something you should go through with. We'll all be there."

"You're not invited," Laurel said with a grin.

"The hell I'm not!" he laughed.

"You're both invited. I already told Mom to make enough food for all of us. Jeff didn't hesitate about the invite. He told me he'd love to meet them and he's looking forward to it."

"And you shouldn't hesitate about being in a serious relationship with him, Liz. Forget who he could've been on the phone with that night. He was with you, not her. He doesn't care about that woman that much otherwise he would've asked her to be his date at the party that night instead of you," Laurel said.

I looked at Marlon. He nodded in agreement and took another sip of his water.

CHAPTER SEVEN

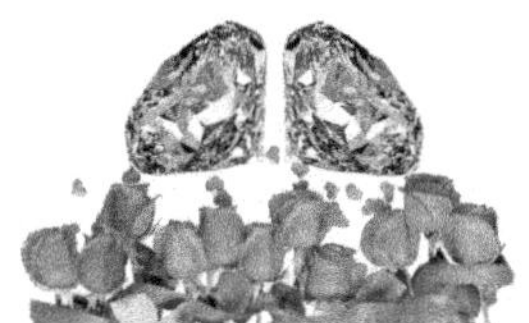

"Dinner was delicious. I can't help but keep saying it. And I see where you got such a nice personality from. Your whole family are very good people," Jeff said, as we drove away from my parents' home after the dinner.

"Thank you," I said with a smile. "They all knew to be on their best behavior. I know you didn't want any special treatment, but people seem to act differently around people like you who have a billionaire status."

"Well, I feel that I'm no different from anyone else, I wish people would see that."

We stared at each other at a stoplight.

"Honestly, I thought the dinner was boring. My family and my brother-in-law normally don't act that well-behaved during dinner any other time. I feel that they were only doing that to impress you, Jeff. I actually couldn't wait until we left, even though Laurel is gonna wanna make me some coffee or tea when I get home and is gonna wanna sit up all night talking about it."

He laughed. "Well, how about we make the night better. You wanna come over to my house?"

I looked at him. This was the first time he'd asked me to come over his house. "Sure," I replied with a smile, as I tried not to show any excitement because I was really looking forward to seeing his house.

Several minutes later we were at his home, and when he opened the door, I had to pick my jaw up off the floor. It was absolutely downright gorgeous. It looked even better than his parents' home. It was fit for a billionaire single man like himself. "This is incredible. I'm continuing to see just how well the other half lives."

He laughed. "Thank you. It was a long road to get here, but I got here sooner than I thought. I thought about downsizing because it's very big for me to only live here, but one day I want a family so I'll stay put for now."

"I'm afraid to walk on this beautiful marble white floor and touch anything," I said, as I looked around in amazement. This was the home of the man who gave me over two-hundred red roses at a concert and he didn't even know me, and we went out the same night for a fourth meal. He bought me a $5,990 cocktail dress and a pair of $2,850 red crystal shoes since I was his date to his parents anniversary party. Then we had lunch the next day, and now we just got done having dinner at my parents' house so they could meet him.

Wow. Just wow.

All of this still felt like a dream to me, and that was the reason why I didn't wanna get too comfortable with all of this, especially now that I was at his house, as I wondered what he had in mind about bringing me here after all.

He led me to his kitchen. "Want anything to drink?"

"I would love a glass of wine."

"Come to my wine cellar," he said with a smile, as he extended out his hand to me.

We held hands as we walked there as I still stared in amazement at his house.

We reached this amazing wine cellar which was surrounded by tall glass and had a touch screen where a code needed to be put in to enter it.

"Wow," I said, as Jeff put in the code. "Never seen a wine cellar that had a code for entering it, but I definitely understand."

He laughed as he opened the glass door. "Yeah, people like to steal, so I definitely have to keep people out of here. The glass is also shatterproof as well as bulletproof."

"Oh, I understand. There must be thousands of bottles in here," I said, as I stared at them. "Bottles seem to reach the ceiling and it's a very tall ceiling. This is incredible. How long have you been collecting wine?"

"For about five years and they're from all over the world as well as from auctions," he replied with a smile as he looked at the bottles.

"Only five years and you have *thousands* of them? I'm sure wine connoisseurs are jealous of this collection!"

He laughed. "Yeah, probably!" He walked over to a certain section. "Here's more of the wine for the ladies right here." He pulled out a bottle. "How about this? It's actually champagne and champagne is a sparkling wine."

"It looks really expensive. I don't even know if I should drink it. The bottle is beautiful—never seen a pink one before so it's very girly—are you sure you wanna open it?"

"It's a special occasion," he said with a smile.

"I agree," I replied with a smile. "What kind is it?"

"It's Armand de Brignac Brut Rose. I have a few bottles of it up here. This is the first one I'll be opening," he replied, as he walked over to a beautiful marble countertop that matched the beautiful marble floors in here. He opened the bottle and poured some into two beautiful Versace wine glasses.

I took a sip. "This is good and even tastes expensive. If you don't mind me asking, how much is a bottle of this so I can buy one myself?"

"$9,800," he said with a grin.

I almost spit out my champagne and nearly dropped the glass! "*$9,800*?! You have got to be kidding, Jeff!" I slowly put my glass down and didn't know if I could take another sip.

"It's okay, Liz," he laughed. "Like I said, I have other bottles. And that's not the most expensive ones I own, not by far."

"I don't even wanna know how much some of these other ones are," I said, as I gazed around the cellar at the hundreds, maybe even thousands, of other bottles. My eyes met up with his again as he smiled at me. "Well, I'm honored that you decided to open a $9,800 bottle of champagne that we could casually have as an after-dinner drink. Thank you again."

"You're always welcome," he replied with a smile. "You wanna take these drinks and go upstairs?"

I nodded with a smile. "That's fine, but I think you should hold my glass because I'm afraid I'll end up tripping over my own feet and dropping it and there goes an expensive glass with $9,800 champagne in it!"

He laughed. "You'll be fine. We'll take the elevator."

I was almost at a loss for words. You hear about houses with elevators and everything, but never did I think I would end up all alone in a single billionaire's house drinking $9,800 champagne and now walking to his elevator to go upstairs to who knows where.

I honestly thought I was dreaming.

We stepped on the elevator.

"This elevator looks better than most luxury hotels," I said, and then sipped some more of my champagne. "Is this the only one?"

"No. I have two more. One is on the other side of the house and the other one is in the kitchen area."

"Where does this one lead to?"

He smiled. "The master bedroom."

I quickly downed some more of my champagne as the elevator door opened to his jaw-dropping master bedroom. I was afraid to step out of it since everything was so luxuriously beautiful and tastefully done. Nothing looked over-the-top like the way some bedrooms looked because the fact was, he could afford anything.

"Wow, your room is beautiful. It looks like a billionaire bachelor's room."

He smiled. "Thank you, Liz."

I didn't know why, but I was so nervous. I didn't expect all of this, and now I had to really wonder why we were up in his bedroom, but I already knew why but didn't wanna even admit it to myself that I knew why.

"Wanna watch some TV?" he asked, as he walked over to a very luxurious spacious area of his room, picked up a remote, and turned on the mounted TV on the wall which looked like it was a hundred inches.

"This TV is beautiful and one of the biggest I've seen. It must be a least a hundred inches."

"Ninety-eight inches, so you were very close," he said with a smile as he sat down on the love seat facing the TV. "Have a seat."

I sat next to him but not too close. I could feel him staring at me. I still held my glass of champagne in my hands even though there was a very expensive-looking table right in front of us that I could put it down on, but I didn't want to accidentally knock over my glass and get it all over the table.

"You can put your glass on the table, it doesn't bite."

I nervously laughed. "Okay," I replied and put my glass on it. "It's just so incredibly beautiful that I didn't know if I could."

"It's just a table. It's meant to have stuff on it besides the flowers in the vase my mom always puts on it. Her and my sister did the floral decorations in my house, by the way."

"And they have beautiful taste. I really like the both of them."

"And they like you, too," he said with a smile.

My eyes met his. "That's great to hear." I looked away fast once again.

"Relax, Liz. I can see that you're nervous. It's just us here."

I laughed and sounded even more nervous. "I guess I'm not hiding my nerves well, am I?"

He smiled. "Not at all. But can I ask why you're so nervous?"

I shook my head. "I really don't know. I guess I can say if anything I just didn't expect to come here tonight."

"You want me to take you home?"

"No," I replied.

"Well, that response was quick!"

We laughed.

I passively watched what was on TV as I tried to get it out of my mind as to why he really brought me up here. I knew that a man didn't bring a woman up to his room to only watch TV; we could've done that downstairs because I saw a few TVs while we were down there, especially in the family room.

I knew it was coming, and it was all just a matter of time.

"Liz."

"Yeah?" I said as I looked at him.

"I just want you to know that I'm not gonna try anything with you, okay? So you can relax. I know what you're thinking."

I nervously laughed once again. "No, I wasn't thinking that," I lied.

He grinned. I knew he wasn't buying a word I'd said. "Okay, that's good to know." He looked at his phone and got up. "I gotta use the bathroom. I'll be back in a minute."

Here we go again, I thought. "Okay," I said with a smile.

I watched him as he walked away from me and disappeared around the first corner. I had no idea where his bathroom was, and this was an incredibly big master bedroom. I stayed seated for a few minutes as I downed the rest of my champagne, and I felt a headache coming on because I drank it a little too fast.

Now I honestly had to use the bathroom.

I got up and went to find where he'd ran off to, and whether he really had to use the bathroom for real was only something he knew. I continued to walk down what it seemed like a long hall and it opened up into the bathroom area which had the most beautiful entry I'd ever seen. I heard the faint sound of the toilet flush and it sounded as if it was a mile away. I froze where I was at because I wasn't sure if there was another toilet in here. I decided to hold it and turned around and began to walk out.

"Liz?"

I looked back as he walked up to me as he put his phone in his pocket. "Yes?"

"You gotta use the bathroom? There's another toilet in here."

"Where?" I asked, because I really had to go and go bad.

"That way around the corner on your right."

"Thank you," I said.

After handling my business in one of the most beautiful bathrooms I'd ever handled my bathroom business in, I walked out of it to him waiting for me.

"Are you okay?"

"Yeah, I'm fine," I replied with a smile. "Are you?"

"Of course," he said.

We walked out of the bathroom.

"That one glass of champagne really made me have to go, plus all of the water I've been drinking."

He smiled at me. "That'll do it."

I felt that he thought I was trying to get out of something with him. But what I really wanted to ask him was why he got up in front of me when he got another call or text and went to his bathroom to talk or text . . . for the second time. This just didn't sit right with me. I wanted to ask, I really did, but I also felt that if I did then he would've perceived me as being nosey and he would've had every reason to think that because when it came to this, I was. I felt that he was already hiding something from me, and if I was gonna have a chance at being in a serious relationship with him then I needed for him to be honest with me because I'd felt that I was honest with him.

We sat back down on the love seat in the suite area and continued to watch TV, and with all of the options we had when it came to what we could watch on TV, I just didn't think he was really interested in watching any of them . . . and neither was I.

"Do you think I'm boring?" I blurted out.

He smiled. "No, I don't think you're boring, Liz, not at all. You weren't expecting to come to my house and I have to admit that I just didn't have anything planned once we got here."

For some reason I believed him.

"I just didn't think I was gonna be asked to come here, that's why I seem so nervous. I've actually been wanting to see your house since seeing your parents' house."

"Well, then I'm glad I asked you did you wanna come here."

I nodded with a smile, and we sat for another minute in silence as we passively watched what was on TV. I was seriously getting bored and I knew he was as well. I picked up my glass of champagne, but it slipped out of my hand and fell to the floor!

"Oh, shit!" I said in a panic as I dove to the floor.

He laughed as he got down on the floor with me. "It's okay, Liz. It was an accident." He looked at the floor and then at the glass. "The glass was empty, obviously. There's nothing on the floor," he said, as he felt over the spot where the glass dropped.

"Yeah, I must be a little tipsy, obviously. I thought I had more in it."

"You want some more?" he asked.

"No, I just can't," I said.

"Okay," he replied with a grin.

We reached for the glass at the same time, and our eyes met each other as we smiled. We held hands. He slowly took the glass from me with his other hand and put it back on the table. We sat back on the couch as we still held hands.

"Are you okay with this?" he asked as he stared at me.

"Yeah, I'm fine," I replied, but in reality, I was scared. I didn't want this to lead to something I wasn't ready for. It was different with him, and I wanted to take it as slow as I could.

He let go of my hand and moved over to me and put his arm around me. I felt a sense of panic come on. It was clearly obvious he was making his move, and it didn't seem to matter what I thought. I knew he finally wanted something for everything he'd given me so far; I was no fool.

"It's okay," he said as he stared at me. "You smell so good. I forgot to tell you that all night."

"Thank you. So do you," I said, and I meant that and now more than ever. I just couldn't be all over him because he had no idea just how moist I was getting *down there*.

I turned to him as he still had his arm around me, smiled and slowly reached my hand up and removed his glasses. I didn't know what made me do it. "Wow. You're gorgeous without your glasses on, too. Ever thought about wearing contacts?"

"Thank you, baby," he said with a smile. "I do have contacts, I just never wear them. It's much easier to reach for my glasses." He leaned into me and we started kissing.

I couldn't believe this was happening.

I abruptly pulled away and jumped to my feet. "I'm sorry."

"What's the matter, Liz?" he asked as he stared at me while he still remained seated. I could tell he was really asking out of concern rather than out of anger that I'd abruptly stopped us kissing. He took his glasses off the table, put them back on, and got on his feet. "Is it me?"

"Absolutely not," I replied. I sighed. "It's just that I'm not ready for this. I thought I would be, but I'm not."

He nodded. "I understand. I told you I wouldn't try and do anything with you tonight and I meant it. I'm sorry if us kissing made you uncomfortable."

I shook my head. "We sound like a bunch of teenagers talking. We're adults."

He grinned. "Yeah, we are, so we should know better and have standards, and I feel that we do know better as well as have standards. Don't you?"

"Yeah, I do." I sighed. "Um, I am a little tipsy and I just don't wanna be in a position where I end up making a choice that I'm gonna end up not being happy about."

"I understand that, Liz. I'll take you home."

I walked into the kitchen where a strong scent of coffee loomed in the air as Laurel sat at the table looking at her phone with the pot in the middle of the table and two mugs. She was obviously waiting for me like she said she would.

"Hey," she said with a big smile, and put her phone down. "How was it?"

"Hey," I replied as I walked over to the table. I sat down while she poured coffee into my mug. I took off my shoes. "How was what?"

"Oh, c'mon, Liz. Don't try to be all coy with me. You know damn well what I'm talking about. You didn't go over Jeff's house just for an after-dinner drink."

"Actually, I did," I replied. "And I had $9,800 champagne."

"Damn!" she said, and then covered her mouth. "I have to remember that Autumn and Marlon are sleeping."

"And I'm getting sleepy, too," I admitted.

"That's why I made the coffee so you could stay up long enough so we could talk about your first time over Jeff's house . . . as well as your first time—"

"Having sex with him?" I cut her off. "No, we didn't have sex, Laurel. *I swear* we didn't. Even though he said he was not gonna make me do anything I didn't wanna do, I just don't know exactly how much of that he meant."

She sipped her coffee as she stared at me. "Wow. I just knew I was gonna hear it all tonight."

"Sorry to disappoint you but nothing happened but us kissing, and I even stopped that."

"Well, that's a start!" she said with a laugh. "And you stopped *that*? What is wrong with you, Liz? You had a chance to make love with a black billionaire who really likes you and you passed up on that chance? That's a chance of a lifetime for most women!"

I sighed. "I didn't wanna do it, Laurel, okay? I need for a man like that to respect me. Any woman, hell, over ninety-nine percent of women would've jumped right in that big, beautiful bed he has and did all kinds of freaky, nasty shit—stuff they would never do with other men—with someone like Jeff, all because of who he is. I just couldn't do it."

She nodded. "And honestly, Liz, I'm glad you didn't. You showed him that you wanted to be respected, and I hope he realizes that."

I sighed once again as I stared down at my coffee mug. "Yeah, I hope so, too, because even though he tried to make it seem like he wasn't, I know a part of him was disappointed because I didn't have sex with him tonight."

"He was," Marlon said as he walked into the kitchen. He got a mug and poured himself a cup of coffee and sat down with us.

Laurel shook her head. "I thought you were asleep."

"I couldn't sleep. I wanted to hear if Liz did anything with Jeff," he said with a grin.

I returned the grin. "Yeah, should've known. Damn, you two. This isn't high school."

They laughed.

"Well, as you heard, I didn't. I take it you feel I did the right thing by not sleeping with him tonight?" I asked him.

"Yeah, you absolutely did the right thing, but eventually he's gonna wanna get some from you, Liz, and the longer you hold off, the less interested he may become in you. Just a heads-up," he warned me.

"Well, if that's the case then he's just used to getting his way with women," Laurel said.

"The man can get as much pussy as he wants and he knows it. There're the women he always gets it from and he doesn't take them seriously at all, and then there're the ones who really never give it to him when he sees them and those are the ones he considers for a serious relationship. I think you know what category you fall into, Liz, and you proved that tonight."

I sighed once again. "Yeah, I may have proved that to him, but I just don't know if he will still wanna talk to me since I didn't have sex with him. I felt like I gave him the impression that he wasn't good enough for me to sleep with when that's not true at all. I know he's Jeff Vick so he can get all the pussy in the world, and I just didn't want him to think I was like all of the other women by giving him what he's always used to getting from a woman when he's alone in his house with her."

Marlon nodded. "Yeah, with a man like Jeff, it's honestly hard to tell if he will continue to be serious about any woman whether or not she's gives him pussy for the first time or not. I'm not gonna say you blew it with him, Liz, but I also can't guarantee you that he will continue to be serious about you."

"Marlon!" Laurel said as she stared at him with anger, and then turned a sympathetic face on to me.

I felt like I sighed for the hundredth time. "Thanks for being honest with me," I said to him. "Oh, and before I forget, he did it again."

Laurel and Marlon looked confused.

"Did what again, Liz?" she asked.

"He got a call or a text and went off to his bathroom which seemed like it was a mile away from where we were at in the suite area of his master bedroom."

"Damn, must be nice," she said.

Marlon nodded in agreement. "Liz, like I told you before, it's none of your business who calls him or texts him. He's definitely seeing other women, but it's clear that he really likes you since it seems as if he's been out with you more than the rest of them lately. I'm sure he hasn't introduced all of the women he meets to his parents and so soon as he did with you at that. Like I said just a minute ago, I can't say that you blew it with him, but I also can't guarantee that he's still gonna be serious about you."

I stared down at my mug. "Thanks again for your honesty."

CHAPTER EIGHT

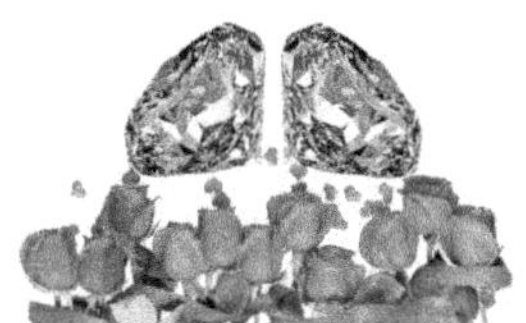

I stood at the counter at Starbucks as I told the barista what I wanted to drink. It was Monday morning and I couldn't wait to take my lunch break and wanted to take it early since it was an unusually slow morning. He told me the total of my drink and I dug in my wallet.

"I got it."

I turned around.

It was my ex-boyfriend Devin!

I managed to crack a smile. "Thanks."

"No problem," he replied with a smile.

After getting my drink, I walked over to my usual table that only had room for two people. I got out my phone to see if I'd gotten any messages, especially from Jeff. I didn't see any. I hadn't spoken to him since that night.

"Mind if I join you?"

I looked up to Devin smiling down at me. "Sure. You paid for my drink."

He sat down right across from me and put his drink on the table. "I didn't think you'd be working anymore since you and the black billionaire are getting serious."

"Nothing is definite, Devin. He didn't say anything about us even being a couple so I'm not counting on anything at this point." And now, since what'd happened the night before since we'd seen each other, I really wasn't counting on it.

"Why not? Isn't this a dream for a woman to be in a relationship with a wealthy man, and especially a billionaire? And you have a black one at that? Wow, Liz, you are way ahead of most women if you're able to get a man like him to marry you."

I gave him a very offensive look because I knew he didn't even realize what he'd said, and this was the way he was and why we were no longer together, amongst a hell of a lot of other things. "Why would I have to *get* someone like Jeff to marry me? It sounds very forced, and that's not how I see my relationship with him. I wanna take things slow and I'm already going through shit in this relationship and it's really not either one of our faults, and nothing has been confirmed about us being a couple."

"Well, I definitely couldn't tell, and I know others couldn't as well."

"Well, I think what everyone could tell was that I didn't go to the concert with him. We met after he gave me those roses."

"Yeah, two-hundred of them," he said, and then took another sip of his drink. "What man gives a woman that many roses that he doesn't even know?"

"One who can afford it," I replied. "And one who knows how to make a very lasting first impression."

He grinned. "Well, I can't argue with that."

"Why are you so concerned about what Jeff and I are doing, huh? You know you sound like one of those gossip rags."

"I just want you to be happy, Liz, that's all."

"I am," I informed him, and took a sip of my drink, but I wasn't a hundred percent about it since I honestly did not know where Jeff and I really stood.

"Well, it's all pure bliss, huh?"

"Yeah, if you say so," I said, and took another sip of my drink.

He gave me a look of skepticism. "You don't seem to believe what you just said."

"Well, what am I supposed to say, Devin? I honestly don't feel like talking about this to you, okay? It just feels awkward and you can understand why. It's clear that we've both moved on from each other with you having a new girlfriend and me seeing someone."

"So, you're confirming that you're seeing him?"

"Why do you care so much? Am I asking you about your girlfriend? I'm not asking because I don't care."

He nodded as he looked down at his drink. "Yeah, you have every right not to care, Liz. I fucked up bad in our relationship; real bad. And since she's pregnant I have some major responsibilities headed my way."

I got up. "I gotta get back to work."

"Let me walk you to your car."

"No, you don't have to walk me anywhere, I'm not a child."

"Liz."

"What?" I asked as I started to get angry, but he still followed me anyway.

Once we walked out of the door, there was a crowd of women around a car in the parking lot. I got closer to see that it was Jeff!

We locked eyes with each other.

"There's your man," Devin said with a smile. "I'm gonna get going because I gotta get back to work since some of us will always have to work."

"Yeah, bye," I said, I still stared at Jeff as he excused himself from the women.

He walked up to me with a smile. "Hey, Liz."

"Hey," I replied with an even bigger smile.

We hugged as I looked right into the cold eyes of the women who surrounded him seconds before. I once again looked around and saw Devin sitting in his car as he was obviously watching me talk to Jeff.

"I thought you were mad at me," I said.

"Why would you say that?" he asked with a grin.

"Because I hadn't heard from you since that night."

He nodded. "I've been busy."

I didn't wanna ask questions . . . for now. "How did you know I was here?"

"You have it on Facebook," he replied.

I laughed. "Yeah, I need to stop being such a creature of habit and posting my whereabouts all the time. But I don't mind that you came to see me."

"Did he come to see you, too?"

I knew he was talking about Devin. "I don't know," I replied, because I honestly didn't, but I had a feeling that he did. "He doesn't work that far from here just like how I don't."

He nodded with a smile. "Well, I don't wanna make you late getting back to work. Can I call you tonight?"

"Sure, I'll love that," I replied with a smile.

"Great. Until then," he said, and lifted up my hand and kissed it.

I blushed. "Thank you."

"Talk to you later."

I watched him as he went back over to his car where those women still stood waiting for him to get done talking to me. I looked around and saw how Devin was still sitting in his car as he was talking on his phone. He then pulled out of the parking lot without waving to me . . . and I didn't care because all I cared about was talking to Jeff later on tonight, and I had a lot of questions to ask him.

CHAPTER NINE

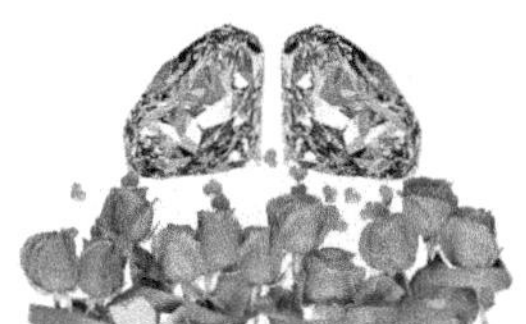

I locked myself in my bedroom like a teenage girl who wanted all the privacy I could get after I had dinner with Laurel, Marlon, and Autumn. I grabbed my phone off of my nightstand to see if Jeff had called me since it was a house rule here not to have any phones at the table during breakfast and dinner, and we all respected it.

Jeff hadn't called.

I sighed with clear disappointment as I sat on my bed with my phone hanging in my right hand, and then stared at it as if I was gonna magically make it ring. I had to wonder why he said he was gonna call me earlier today when he hadn't by now. Just how much did he really like me? I knew I was overthinking everything because he came to see me during my lunch break, so I knew he obviously still did like me. I just felt that someone like Jeff was one in a billion—worth more than what he was worth—so I didn't want the slightest chance of ruining anything with him. But it seemed as if he was hiding a lot of things from me.

My phone lit up to Jeff's picture smiling back at me. I answered it in record time.

"Hey, Jeff," I said, as I tried hard not to sound relieved that he'd called.

"Hey, Liz," he said. "Sorry I didn't call you earlier. I was at my parents' house having dinner."

"That's okay," I said with a smile. *As long as you called when you said you were going to,* I thought.

"So, do you have any plans right now?"

"Not really. I was just gonna watch some movies on YouTube since I recently got a 4K TV."

"Sounds great. But I got an even better idea."

I perked up. "What's that?"

"You wanna watch them over here on my TV?"

"I thought you'd never ask!"

We laughed.

"I'll be right over."

"I just can't get over the beauty of this home. It literally looks like a royal palace," I said, as Jeff gave me a Canada Dry since I had to drive home because I had to work the next day. He sat on the couch next to me while we sat in the family room.

"Thank you, Liz. It's a lot for one person but I know I wanna have a family someday so I wanted to be prepared ahead of time and have a nice home."

I took a sip of my drink. "And it's nice to know that when you do have a family that they will automatically be living their best lives possible."

He continued to smile at me. "Yeah, they will."

I smiled back as I turned my attention back to the TV. I started to feel uncomfortable once again because I didn't know what he wanted me over here for.

Was it to give me a second chance to submit to him?

What if it was and I didn't do it?

I honestly tried not to think about all of this since I wanted to talk because I felt like there were so many unanswered questions when it came to him.

"So, your ex showed up at Starbucks as well, huh?" he asked with a grin. I could tell he was trying to get a conversation going, but this was not what I wanted to talk about.

I rolled my eyes. "Yeah, he did. He usually goes there a lot. He paid for my drink thinking that was gonna make up for all of the shit he's done to me. Then he had the audacity to tell me that his current girlfriend is pregnant; like I really care," I said, and took a sip of my drink.

He nodded with a smile. "Well, I'm glad *you* didn't end up pregnant by him."

"Not without a wedding ring on my finger," I replied. "And as you see, I never got it. Five years and I never got it. But he gets this chick pregnant and has only been with her for a few months. He knew I strongly believed in the marry-before-you-carry rule, and I still do. But it's clear he didn't wanna marry me much less start a family, so I said fuck it and him."

He laughed and then took a sip of his bottled water. "Well, I'm glad it didn't work out between the two of you because then we would've never met."

"Yeah, me too. I just told myself that there was a reason why he never asked me to marry him and we ended our relationship, and that's because there was someone better out there for me."

"You're absolutely right, Liz."

We looked at each other and smiled.

"So, are *you* seeing anyone right now?" I had to ask.

He grinned. "Only you. That's if you wanna call us seeing each other."

"I'm not objecting to it!" I said with excitement.

He laughed. "I was hoping you wouldn't! My parents and sister really like you. They were asking me when I had dinner with them earlier today when I was I gonna bring you back over to their house, and Jenelle wanted to know when I was I gonna bring you to hers. I just told them that it will be up to you since you work and everything."

"I would love to see them again anytime," I said with a big smile. "They are some of the nicest people I've ever met."

"And they told me they didn't think women like you existed

anymore. In your thirties and have never been married with no children. They told me not to let you get away."

I smiled big! "You're kidding, Jeff," I said in a calm demeanor. I didn't want him to think I was getting overexcited about what his family had said about me, but it was definitely great to hear!

"No, I'm not, Liz. They really like you. More than any of the other women I've been involved with. I will never tell you anything that isn't true."

"That's something I don't hear often," I said with a grin and then took another sip of my drink. "All my ex did was lie to me, another reason why we're not together anymore. But I didn't come over here to talk about him so let me shut up."

He laughed. "It's okay. It's clear you still have a lot of things to get off your chest about him."

"Yeah, and it's too bad I couldn't get him off of other women's chests."

He laughed hard! "You're funny, Liz, seriously. I love a woman with a sense of humor; keeps me going."

I smiled. "Glad to hear it." My smile disappeared into a serious look of concern. "I have to be honest with you, Jeff."

"Honest with me about what?"

I sighed. "I just didn't know if I was gonna hear from you again since, you know, what happened over here the last time."

"You mean what *didn't* happen," he said with a grin.

I returned the gesture. "Yeah, you're right, what *didn't* happen. I just didn't know if you would've respected me if I'd done anything or you were expecting me to do something because of all of things you've given me so far. I just didn't know."

He nodded with a smile as he stared passively at the TV. His eyes met back up with mine. "I understand. And it's great that you do think about that. It shows me—and especially yourself—that you have a lot of respect for yourself, and that's a quality I always look for in a woman."

"Yeah, nothing is worth me losing my self-respect over. I see and hear women doing stuff all the time which tells the world that they have no self-respect. I just didn't want you to think I was that type who didn't."

"Self-respect is ageless. Like I said, it's the one thing a woman should never compromise. I admit to having flings with a lot of women who didn't have any, and they showed me they didn't. It shouldn't be any surprise to anyone why I'm still single, but it is to a lot of people."

"Actually, it's not a surprise to me. You're being careful by not getting seriously involved with the majority of the women you meet. I just notice that women seem to swarm you every time you're around."

"It's the cars."

I laughed. "Jeff, you know damn well it's your billionaire status."

He nodded with a smile. "I know. And that's why I wanted to find someone who knew nothing about me; someone who didn't see me for the first time in one of my cars or whatever. I am who I am and eventually they're gonna find out about my status. I knew you didn't know anything about me when we first met and I loved that."

"Yeah, I can say with a clear conscience that I'd never heard of you until we met and didn't know you were a billionaire until all of those gossip reporters showed up at my house the next day after we met."

"I'm still sorry about that. I wanted to tell you myself, but they beat me to it. To this day I wish they wouldn't have done that."

"Well, that's the media for you. Always meddling in people's business, especially the gossip ones. It's who they are; comes with the territory."

He nodded. "It unfortunately does."

I continued to stare at him. "Um, I know I shouldn't be asking this."

"Asking me what?"

I turned my attention to the TV even though I didn't care what was on. "I just wanna know if, you know, you're seeing other women?"

He turned away from me with a huge grin. "Not recently, no."

I didn't know how I should've taken this, or whether or not I should've believed him. We weren't exclusive to each other so I actually couldn't get mad if he was seeing other women. "I'm sorry for asking."

"No problem, Liz. I actually haven't had a girlfriend since Karis, and that was well over a year ago. Yes, I've seen women since then, but it's been nothing serious. I said I wanted to settle down eventually, but like I told you, I wanna settle down with the right woman."

I nodded with a smile. "And I wanna settle down with the right man." I shook my head. "I get so jealous of Laurel at times because she married the right man even though I know I shouldn't. I just feel that us meeting each other is still a dream to me so if it is, please don't wake me up."

He laughed. "It's no dream, Liz. Like I told you before, it was something about you at the show. I just couldn't take my eyes off of you the whole time you were there. You looked so beautiful but at the same time so sad and lonely."

"You're right, I was," I said, and then took another sip of my drink. "But you took that night and turned it around instantly even though it was at the end of the show. I couldn't believe everything was happening as it was happening. I felt I was watching some other women and not myself. I said that this was not my type of luck."

He laughed once again. "I'm glad I made the night as beautiful as you are after all."

I blushed. "You sure did."

We started kissing . . . and I didn't stop him.

"Are you okay?" he asked as we still kissed, and slowly went down to my neck as well as my décolleté.

"Yes," I replied as I started breathing heavy because this was feeling so good. It was something I wanted. Something I needed.

"You wanna go upstairs to my bedroom? We'll be more comfortable there."

I nodded with a smile because I knew what he wanted this to lead to and I felt comfortable enough to have it lead to this as well.

We got on the elevator leading right to his master bedroom and began kissing again. We started becoming more sexually aggressive with each other as I jumped up on him while we still kissed each other all over and we were going at it so hard his glasses were almost knocked off. As we still went at it hard as the elevator slowly made its way up to his bedroom, I felt like I was reenacting the scene in the classic movie *Fatal Attraction*.

The elevator door opened and he carried me over to his bed while we still kissed each other like neither one of us hadn't done anything like this in a long time and was waiting for this moment to become a reality between us . . . and it finally had.

I pulled down his pants and began giving him what I knew he was waiting for.

"Damn, baby!" he said with a big smile on his face, and moaned until he was satisfied. "Never had it done that good! That was on point for real! You sucked the soul out of me!"

I laughed hard as he put on a condom. "Never heard that before! It's been a long time since I've done it. Didn't know if I could still do it right."

"It was done more than just right," he said, and slowly went inside of me. "Does this feel good, baby?" he asked me as he breathed heavy while moving back and forth.

"Feels just right," I replied as I breathed heavy as well, and tried not to laugh because he still had his glasses on. I turned over and he went inside of me from behind and moved so fast my moaning echoed and vibrated throughout this room. This was clearly what we were both waiting for, and I felt that it was worth the wait.

Minutes later, I was in his arms.

"So, if I may ask, how did I do?" he asked, as he had his right arm around me and was *still* wearing his glasses.

"You were great," I honestly replied.

"Great to hear. And so were you. Damn, you feel so good!"

I laughed. "I was hoping you'd say that! But can I ask you something?"

"What is it?"

"How the hell did you keep your glasses on the whole time we were having sex?"

He laughed hard! "I'm so used to wearing them that I don't even think about it. They seem to just stay stuck on my face."

I laughed once again. "Yeah, it seems like it!"

"So, we can both agree that our first time with each other was memorable?"

"Absolutely memorable," I replied with a smile. But I still had questions. "Um, Jeff?"

"Yeah?" he asked as his eyes were closed while he still had his arm around me.

"You weren't mad or anything that it *kind of* took us a while to do this? You know, because of all of the nice stuff you've given me. I actually thought you were gonna wanna do this that first night I met you at the concert."

"It didn't even cross my mind, Liz, it honestly didn't." He turned and looked at me. "I didn't expect anything from you, and you know why?"

"Why?" I asked in a surprised tone.

"Because I'm the one who initiated everything. I'm the one who took the chance on you without knowing a thing about you. I'd hoped that you were gonna turn out to be the beautiful woman that you are, and I was right . . . but I didn't know until I introduced myself to you."

I smiled. "Yeah, you never can tell how someone is gonna be until you actually meet them. I wasn't raised to want for nothing. I was raised to have all of the self-respect I can have and to treat people the way I want to be treated, as well as to work for what I want. I still can't believe all of this, Jeff. I honestly didn't think I was gonna meet another man this soon, and not only this soon, a billionaire at that. Now that never, *ever* crossed my mind."

He smiled with a nod. "And that's what makes our relationship so good, huh?"

"Yeah, you're right. It's always so full of surprises already."

"And I love surprising you."

We kissed once again.

"Have you ever done that before?"

He gave me a confused look. "Done what before?"

"Gave a woman that many roses and didn't even know her?"

He grinned. "No, I've never done that before, Liz. That was the first time."

"Wow, I really feel special." And I meant that.

"And that's exactly how I wanted you to feel. I love going to concerts, it's my thing. I just love the atmosphere and the live music and all. It's just that I haven't been to many where they've given out roses like that, and even the ones I've been to I'd never seen any women that I wanted to give even one rose to, much less two hundred. As they say, Liz, it was something about you."

"I really feel special," I repeated. "I just never thought I would be this happy and this involved with someone else so soon, and it's all worth it."

"Glad to hear it."

We kissed once more.

His phone rang. He took it off the nightstand and looked at it. "I'll be right back."

Here we go again, I thought, but nodded with a smile as I watched his beautiful naked body get out of bed and disappear around the corner.

I was tempted to follow him like what I'd done the last time I was over here. I just had sex with him for the first time, and I felt that he was still keeping secrets from me. I honestly felt like someone he just wanted to have this kind of fun with and then he'd find someone who he felt was better and move on to her, and give her roses and expensive dresses and shoes, let her meet his parents and sister—all that. I hope I was wrong. Everyone had secrets, but I just didn't know if I could continue to sit here and act as if I didn't know what he could possibly be doing and most of all if I did know what he was doing, I didn't care.

CHAPTER TEN

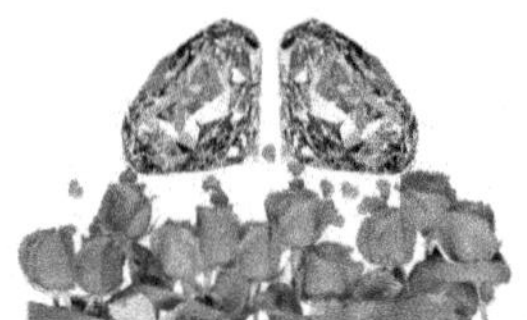

"Good morning."

I woke up to Jeff smiling at me with a tray in his hands. I looked at the time. "OH, SHIT!" I said as I jumped up out of bed.

"What's wrong?" he asked, as he sat the tray on an accent table.

"I'm late for work!" I informed him, as I frantically tried to put on my clothes. I tripped and fell to the floor as I tried to get my left leg in my jeans. I started to laugh as I stayed on the floor.

He joined me. "I'm glad you were able to laugh about this."

I sighed. "I'm just gonna have to call in sick. And believe me, I take my sick days seriously. I clearly overslept. It's like you went to the bathroom last night and that's the last time I saw you, and now I wake up and you're holding a tray of food for me."

He nodded with a smile. "Yeah, I thought I'd make you breakfast in bed since I didn't wanna wake you since you were sleeping so soundly. You should've told me you had to go to work today; I would've made sure you got home much earlier last night."

"I didn't realize just how tired I was," I said.

"I wore you out, huh?" he asked with a sexy grin.

"That's an understatement!"

We laughed as I texted my boss and told her I wasn't gonna be in today because I was sick. She immediately texted back and told me that was fine and to get well. I actually felt bad. "Well, I have the day off."

"That's good. You still want your food?"

I smiled. "Of course."

We sat in the suite area of his bedroom as I ate my breakfast—silver dollar pancakes and a bowl of fresh berries with a glass of orange juice and a cup of coffee.

"This is so good, Jeff. Do you always cook?"

"Not always. I love to eat out more than I cook even though I do have an on-call chef."

"Must be nice," I said, and took a sip of my orange juice. "So, where did you tip off to after you had that phone call?"

He grinned. "I was still here, Liz. By the time I got back in here, you were kinda snoring so I didn't wanna wake you up."

I laughed. "Yeah, I was tired! Great sex does that to you!"

"It definitely does!"

He smiled at me as he continued to watch me eat. I still felt like he wasn't telling me something, but was it really my business to find out?

"So, since you're pretty much playing hooky from work, wanna spend the day here?"

"I thought you'd never ask!"

We laughed and then kissed.

After I was done with breakfast, we tried to figure out what we wanted to do since I couldn't be caught anywhere outside of here, and I didn't mind spending the day in a palace; I didn't think anyone would.

"Wanna go swimming?" he suggested.

"I don't have a swimsuit here," I reminded him.

"My sister has a lot of them in a spare room she has here when I have pool parties here. You two look like you're about the same size." He pulled me up off the couch. "C'mon."

Minutes later, I shuffled through Jenelle's beautiful, extensive swimwear collection. I tried not to gasp as I flipped over tags to some swimsuits being over $500, $700, and even over $1K. Yeah, all tags still attached.

Must be nice.

"Um, maybe you should call her and let her know I wanna wear one of her swimsuits. They're all so beautiful I honestly don't know which one to choose."

"It's entirely up to you, Liz. And Jenelle doesn't care at all so there's no need for me to call her. She has about a hundred times more at her home. She probably forgot she had these over here."

"Okay, if you say so!" I said, and picked out a beautiful Versace red bikini with Greca chain gold straps on the top and bottom—and each piece had a separate price. $625 for the top and $595 for the bottoms. I tried it on. "I've never worn a bikini this beautiful and especially this expensive."

"It looks beautiful on you," he said with a smile.

Minutes later, we were in his beautiful, luxurious pool completed with a huge waterfall and dual slides on each side of it. I stared around at just how beautiful this backyard was; looked like a tropical paradise. I honestly *still* felt that I was dreaming.

"Can I get some pictures and videos of you?" he asked with a smile.

"As long as you don't post them today. Remember, I'm supposed to be sick at home from work, instead, I feel like I'm on vacation on an island!"

"Okay, I won't. I almost forgot," he said with a laugh.

"Yeah, it's very easy to, especially for me!" I said, and then dove underneath the water and swam to the edge of the pool where the slides were. I got out and he followed me.

"Can I slide down with you?" he asked with that sexy grin.

"I would've been mad if you didn't," I said.

We laughed as we climbed up the ladder to the slide on the right side of the waterfall. He got behind me, held me with both arms, and we slid down and splashed once again into the water. I felt like a child who'd never had this much fun, and in reality, it was a long time since I had.

We embraced each other once again.

"I'm glad you're having fun, Liz."

"I really truly am, Jeff. I haven't had this much fun in I can't tell you how long. I honestly can't."

"Glad to hear it."

We began kissing, and once again, I didn't stop him.

I felt his hand slowly pull my bikini bottom down, and the next thing I knew it was floating in the water. I slightly moaned as I felt him slowly go inside of me.

"Are you okay?" he asked with a smile.

"Yes," I replied.

He started to move faster and I moved right along with him, and we were moving so fast the water crashed and splashed like Tsunami waves all around us.

We did it again.

I let out the little breath I had left as I laid my head on his shoulder. "Damn, that was fuckin' good—no, great. Never have I had sex in a pool before and a paradisiac one at that."

He smiled as he held me. "Then I'm glad you said your first time in one was great . . . and it was. Just like last night." He slowly lifted my chin. "Liz, I've had such a good time with you last night and just now. I've never connected to a woman like the way I've connected to you. Like I told my parents and sister last night, you make me very happy, and it always makes me feel good when you say how happy you are when we're together."

"I will never lie to you, Jeff."

"And I will never lie to you."

Hours later, it was finally time for me to go home. I got in my car and tried to start it as he stood outside of my window. It wouldn't start. "I don't believe this shit!" I said with full-fledged anger and embarrassment. "It's doing it again."

"Here, let me try," he said.

He couldn't get it to start either. "The battery is dead. Did you leave anything on?"

"I don't think so," I said, but I wasn't sure. "It's an old car. From 2004 and I got it used. It's just a piece of shit but I need it to get me to and from work. It did this before, in fact, a few times. Looks like I would've had to call in sick after all since my car probably wouldn't have started at that time either. I'll call a tow. That's what I have insurance for."

"When they get here, I'll drive you home."

I smiled. "Thanks, Jeff."

Several minutes later I walked through the door to Laurel putting dishes in the dishwasher.

"Hey," I said, and sat at the table.

She grinned big at me. "Now *I know* a lot went down last night *and* today! You didn't even call me to tell me you were gonna stay over at Jeff's last night."

"I didn't know I was, either. After we had sex—yes, we had sex and it was great—I fell asleep when he had left the room to take a call."

"Uh, oh!" she said, and then started the dishwasher. "You want some coffee?"

"No, that's okay. It'll keep me up all night. And that's just it. I fell asleep and didn't wake up until this morning. I was gonna come back here last night. He said he would've made sure I got here last night if I told him I had to work, but it was like as soon as I got to his house, I forgot all about having to work today. I feel like I step into a fantasy world when I'm at his home. I bet he doesn't think that house is even half as big and beautiful as I think it is."

"Yeah, he probably doesn't because that's just the life he lives. But since you didn't call me so I had to call you, how was your hooky day from work?"

I laughed. "Beautiful."

"How was your head game?" Marlon asked with a huge grin as he walked into the kitchen.

"Marlon!" Laurel said with a laugh.

"On point," I replied with pride. "That's what Jeff told me. I only did it to him last night. He said I sucked the soul out of him."

They burst into laughter!

"Yeah, Liz! You still got it!" Marlon said as he still laughed.

"Yeah, I told him it was a long time since I'd done it so I didn't know if I still had it, but I do. But I didn't do it to him when we had sex again in his paradisiac pool."

"Wow, sounds sexy!" Laurel said.

"It was. Best hooky day I've ever had. From work, school, anywhere!"

We all laughed.

"Well, I'm tired. And I may have to have one of you give me a ride to work tomorrow because I don't know if my car is gonna start. It's acting up again. It wouldn't start when I left his house that's why I had to get it towed here."

"We got you, Liz, you know that," Marlon said with a smile as Laurel nodded.

"Thanks, guys," I replied, and went up to my bedroom as I thought about the night before and a day I would never forget.

CHAPTER ELEVEN

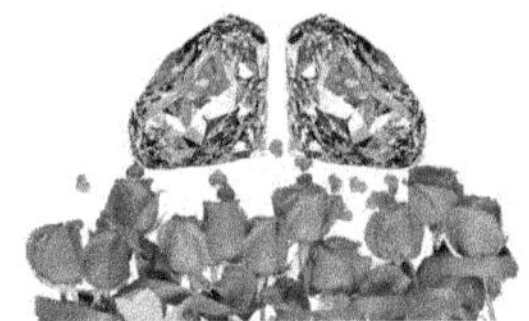

Back to reality.

I opened up the garage door to overcast skies as I couldn't stop thinking about my night and day that I'd spent with Jeff. It was beautiful, magical, a true fantasy for every woman out there. I honestly didn't want it to end. But for now, this was my reality. I wasn't even his girlfriend, just an intimate friend, and I didn't even wanna think about the possibility of the fact that he could have someone else out there because a man like him pretty much always had side women. Always.

I walked between Laurel and Marlon's cars since they always had their cars parked in the garage and mine was always out in the driveway. I stopped cold.

My car was gone!

I ran back into the house!

"LAUREL! MARLON! MY CAR! MY CAR IS GONE!" I screamed in a panic. "SOMEONE STOLE MY FUCKIN' CAR!"

"Calm down, Liz! You have insurance!" Laurel said as her and Marlon ran downstairs and out the door with me.

We ran outside of the garage and stopped cold.

There was a beautiful white Porsche Panamera sitting in the driveway with a big pink bow on it!

"OH, MY GOD!" Laurel screamed! "THANK YOU, HONEY! THANK YOU!" she said to Marlon as she jumped on him and smothered him with kisses.

"Ummmm," Marlon said, as he still stared at the car in shock.

Jeff appeared! "Good morning, everyone."

"JEFF!" I said with a big smile.

"WHAT?!" Laurel said, and immediately let go of Marlon!

"Surprise," Jeff said to me in a calm voice, but held a huge grin on his face at the same time since he'd witnessed Laurel think the car was hers from Marlon!

I stood in shock. "This is *mine*?! You bought this car for *me*?!"

"It's absolutely for you, Liz. I bought it online last night when I got home from dropping you off. The dealership told me they just got it in that day. Brand new. I hope you like it," Jeff replied with a smile.

I still stood in shock. I couldn't believe this. "This is crazy, Jeff. This is too beautiful and too much."

"Nothing is ever too much," Jeff said with a smile. "Now you don't have to worry about how you're gonna get to and from work."

"You're right about that! And this car is what the top doctors drive. I'm just an admin coordinator."

"You don't have to be a top doctor to drive this car, Liz," Jeff said.

Marlon walked slowly around the car, checking it out. He looked at the window sticker. "$128,000. Damn, Liz. You're one lucky woman."

I looked at Jeff as he smiled back at me. "I sure am." We embraced with a kiss. "Thank you so much, Jeff. I'll never forget this."

"I gotta get Autumn up and fix her breakfast. Nice seeing you again, Jeff. Excuse me," Laurel said, and turned around and walked back into the house.

Jeff and I looked at Marlon.

"Shit, don't look at me. She should've never assumed anything. Liz, you said *your car* was missing, not hers. What did she reasonably expect?" he said. "Let me get inside and get ready for work. Nice seeing you again, man."

"Nice seeing you too, man," Jeff said, as him and Marlon shook hands.

Jeff looked at me as he continued to grin.

"Yeah, I'm gonna hear it about this later on. I may wanna stay with you tonight."

"You're always welcome, Liz. In fact, I'll love it."

We kissed again as a beautiful Porsche SUV came up in the driveway.

"Who's that?" I asked.

"The owner of the Porsche dealership. He's here to show you the ends and outs of your new car. Do you have time?"

"Yes, I do."

"I don't know why you're still pissed off about Liz's new car not being yours, Laurel. I'm not gonna deal with this shit from you. The car you have is just fine and not even five years old," Marlon said.

"Well, how did you think I was gonna act? Liz didn't say anything about how Jeff bought her a new car," she said.

"She didn't know she was getting it, that's why. That's what surprises are for. He obviously took her old car and replaced it with a new one. Damn, you don't need to be so pissed off about this. You should be happy for your sister that she's in a relationship with Jeff. He's the rarest of the rare. You knew that if they were still getting together like the way they are that the gifts were gonna start getting bigger and bigger."

"Yeah, whatever. When was the last time you bought me anything that nice? And you're my husband!"

"And I can ask you the same damn thing!" he snapped back. "Like I can really afford to buy you a *$128,000* car on a whim and have it delivered here as a surprise for you just because your current car won't start, Laurel! Be fuckin' for real!"

I stood around the corner as I listened to all of this. Just as I expected, they were *still* arguing about it. "Hey," I said with a smile as I finally appeared from around the corner.

"Hey, Liz," Marlon said as he stood with both of his hands pressed on the edges of the kitchen island counter.

Laurel shot me a glare. "Y'all are on your own for dinner tonight. Autumn's at ballet class and I just don't feel like cooking." She left the kitchen.

Marlon looked at me with a smile. "How's your new ride?"

"I still can't believe he bought me something so beautiful and expensive. I was actually scared to drive it since it rained on the way to work and on the way home today. And I just wanna let you know that I didn't ask for this car. I had no idea that he was gonna buy it for me. It was just as much as a surprise to me as it was to the two of you."

"Yeah, especially to her," he said.

I sighed. "She shouldn't be mad at you, Marlon. Her car is just fine. I don't know why she thought that you got her a car that expensive."

"I don't know why she thought that either, Liz, but that's your sister for you. I thought she would be happy that he did buy you something that nice. That was very nice of him. You rocked the shit out of his world for those two days, huh?"

I laughed. "I would like to say I did, but never did I think he would give me something like this. I think it's way overly generous. I'm not even his girlfriend. Most men can't even and will never be able to buy their wives that kind of car, much less girlfriends, and even much less someone he's just seeing like me."

"Tell me about it," Marlon said. He got a beer out of the refrigerator. "I'm gonna watch a game before I get to work. Congrats on the car again, Liz. You deserve it."

"Thank you, Marlon," I said with a smile. "And Jeff told me that any of you can drive it at any time."

"I'll *definitely* take you and him up on that!" he said with a smile. "See you later."

I felt so bad for him. Laurel knew damn well she was being an overacting bitch about this. She had a great husband and a great child. Her life wasn't perfect, but for her to be upset that he didn't get the car for her and a man I felt I was at least seeing got something that expensive for me because he could clearly afford to? Well, I felt that she was showing her true colors. She was raised much better than that.

I walked upstairs to my bedroom. I stopped cold in my tracks when I heard Laurel on the phone.

"Yeah, Mom. It looks like Liz is really trying her hardest to keep Jeff. You saw the car he bought her today. She *claims* that she didn't ask for it, but I seriously doubt that because that old piece of shit she used to have was always conking out on her. Hey, I ain't mad at her for getting all that she can out of him because the bottom line is that someone with his status always has other women around. Always. So she better enjoy it while it lasts."

I continued to walk to my room as tears welled up in my eyes. She was sounding like a hater than like my own sister. She was my best friend. She was the last one I thought would act like this. She wasn't hating over the dress and shoes he bought me when I went as his date to his parents anniversary party—or was she? But it was very clear now since the gifts had gotten bigger from Jeff—something that her husband couldn't afford to get her—she wanted to turn on me and start acting like all of these other hating-ass women out here that didn't like the fact that Jeff and I were seeing each other.

I closed the door to my room and got out an overnight bag and started putting clothes and shoes in it. I just couldn't stay here tonight.

CHAPTER TWELVE

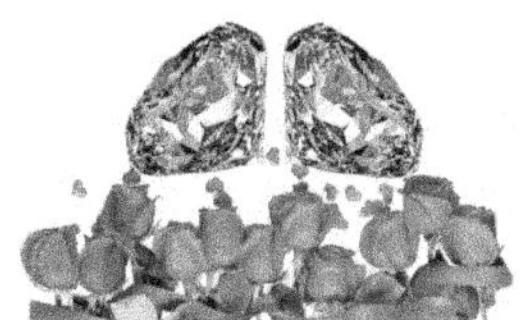

"And she was the one who really loved the fact that I started seeing you. I mean, right from the start she told me not to blow it with you, and now she's acting like a hater just because she thought my new car was hers from Marlon," I said, as I sat on the sofa next to Jeff in his family room while staring down at my cup of hot tea.

"I'm really sorry to hear this, Liz. I didn't mean to cause any trouble this morning. I know how it is to have haters, believe me, and some of the biggest ones can be your own family members."

"Yeah, it's always like that. But it's like she was so happy for me. I just can't believe what I overheard her telling our mom, that 'I'm trying my hardest to keep you' and 'I better enjoy it while it lasts.'"

He shook his head. "Damn, Liz. I don't know what to say except that it sounds like sudden jealousy to me. It happens with siblings all the time."

"But that's just it. She has nothing to be jealous of. She's married to a great man and they have a great child. And she's been wanting me to find happiness once again ever since my last relationship. I guess she just didn't think I would end up with someone like you since you're the rarest of the rare, and I'm still seeing you since you can get any woman you want."

"That doesn't mean I want them, Liz, you know that. There're very few women out there that are worth my time."

I nodded. "So it's safe to say that I'm one of them?"

"You're absolutely one of them," he said with a smile.

I smiled big in return. "Thanks, Jeff."

We kissed.

"You know, I never really asked you what was your type? Why did you pick me out of all of the other women you could have?"

"Well, my type is definitely someone like you. A woman with class that has respect for herself and others; not a thirst-trap attention whore. Someone who has respect for me when I have it for them. Someone who doesn't take things for granted; doesn't act like someone owes her something and feels entitled to any and everything just because I can afford to give her any and everything. Of course, I didn't know any of this for sure about you when I saw you at the concert, Liz. I just saw a beautiful woman who I couldn't believe didn't have a man sitting next to her. I went on instinct and took the chance."

"And here we still are," I said with a smile.

"We sure are."

We kissed once again.

"Once I started to get to know you, you were even better than I imagined. You don't have any children, and that's one of my main criteria. It's not optional to me. I've had to turn down many women—way too many to count—because of this, but it's my requirements and criteria. I don't want a woman who has already given a man or men, the greatest gift that she can give him, and that's a child. It means too much to me. They wanna have babies by losers but now want a leader, and I'm not the leader they're gonna get."

"Exactly, Jeff. And I don't blame you one single bit, especially a man with your status. Men have to be careful with the women they get involved with, but a man like you has to be extra, extra careful."

He took a sip of his drink. "You're right, Liz. My mom always says, 'If she already has a baby or babies then she can't be your lady.'"

"Wow, your mom isn't playing, huh?"

"No, she isn't. Not at all. My dad says the same thing, too, as well as my sister. They told me to never take care of something that isn't mine."

"And no one can get all up in their feelings about that, either. They made a choice they can't change and they have to live with it for the rest of their lives. We need to have more spirit of discernment out here. People are just sleeping with anyone and women are allowing themselves to get pregnant by just anyone. It's just ridiculous. And even the ones who think they know the man or woman they're sleeping with all the time find out the hard way when a baby is born and that man wants to have nothing to do with her or that child. Or the man finds out just how fucked up some woman really is who had a child by him. Now he's connected to her for life. No spirit of discernment on either of their parts."

"Absolutely right, Liz. I'm not responsible of any women's children—the fathers of those children are. I don't know why these women see me as their king or something that's gonna sweep them off of their feet and put them and their kid or kids in this home so they can all live a fairytale lifestyle. I'm not the one. I'm not responsible for anyone's lifestyle but my own. I don't care if a woman has one or ten or twenty kids, I don't want any of them. Too bad, I'm not their man, move on. Should've made better choices then they would've had better options, and one of those better options would've been me. Never make a choice where your options will be compromised for the rest of your life. Of course, I'm not trying to sound arrogant, just speaking the truth."

"And the truth hurts and hurts bad. Never feel bad about telling the truth. When I hear you say these things directly it makes me very glad I made better choices than most women and now I have one of the best options—you."

He smiled with a nod. "You're right, Liz. I knew you weren't like most of these women out here."

"No, I'm not," I replied with pride. "But good for you, Jeff. Make no apologies for how you are and what your criteria is and never compromise it for anyone. You were raised with morals and values and that's why you live the life that you live."

"And that's why I want someone who feels the same way I do to share it with. And it all starts with her being my girlfriend."

I nodded with a smile.

He stared at me with a smile. "I hope this doesn't seem too fast, Liz, but I want you to be my girlfriend."

My mouth dropped in shock. "WHAT?! Stop playing with me, Jeff."

"I'm not playing with you, Liz. I want you to be my girlfriend. I haven't had a girlfriend in almost two years. I normally wouldn't ask a woman this fast, but everything just feels so right with you; right with us. I didn't buy you the car to try and persuade you to say yes, just wanna let you know that."

"Yes," I said with a smile as tears welled up in my eyes.

He smiled as he let out a sigh of relief. "I don't know why I was so nervous in asking you. I just never know what a woman is gonna say until I ask. I didn't know if you were still stuck on your ex or not."

"Fuck no!" I said, as tears streamed down from my eyes.

He laughed hard! "I gotta go get something. Stay here."

It was official.

I was Jeff Vick's girlfriend!

Only one of two black billionaires in the world in his age range, and the other one was married. I thought I was dreaming.

Jeff returned to the room with a beautifully wrapped gift in his hand. "This is for you."

"Uh, oh!" I said, as I took the box from him. "Christmas came early!"

He laughed. "Yeah, I thought since this was special I wanted to have it wrapped."

"It's so beautifully wrapped it's like I don't even wanna open it. Who wrapped it?"

"My mom. I don't know how she does it, but she wraps gifts better than the people who get paid for it for the holidays which is what she lives for."

I laughed as I carefully unwrapped it. "Yeah, so does my mom!" I took off all of the wrapping that exposed a beautiful black box with the designer's name on it . . . .

Judith Leiber.

"Holy!" I said, before I opened the box. "You got me something from *Judith Leiber*?! Oh, my God! This is one of my favorite designers even though I don't own anything from it."

"Now you do," he replied with a smile.

I opened up the box, took the small item out of it and out of its dustcover, and gasped as I pulled out an absolutely jaw-dropping sparkling mini-bag in the shape of a beautiful red rose as the beautiful red and green crystals danced under the dim lights in this room. "This is too beautiful beyond words, Jeff. Thank you so much."

"You're welcome, baby. I wanted to get you a rose that will last forever because I know the roses I gave you that night haven't."

"No, they didn't! I kept them as long as I could!"

We laughed as I still held this absolutely beautiful jeweled bag in my hand. This was stunning; a true work of art. I couldn't believe he gave this to me as a gift.

I pulled out the beautiful glistening gold straps as well as the price tag—*$4,995*. "Wow, Jeff. I've never had a bag this expensive and it's not one I would carry every day."

He laughed with a nod. "No, it's not an everyday bag, but we'll be going to some nice places where I think you'd like to carry it to."

"Oh, without a doubt!" I said as I still stared at it in amazement. It was a true work of art in every sense of the word.

"Can I get some pictures of you with it?"

"Sure, I'd love that."

As he took pictures of me holding my latest gift, I smiled as I couldn't believe I was actually his girlfriend, and I knew eventually everyone was gonna find out.

"So, when do we tell everyone that we're officially a couple?" I asked.

"Whenever you're ready. I'll let you decide."

"I'm ready now!" I said with excitement.

We laughed.

"Well, in honor of you accepting my asking you to be my girlfriend, how about we go out to dinner tonight? It's still early. I'll let you pick the place."

"Sounds great to me, and I'm carrying my beautiful new bag."

"Can't blame you for that, Liz. It's beautiful and looks beautiful on you."

"Thank you, baby. And you know what? I actually brought my red crystal Jimmy Choo's, the ones I wore to your parents wedding anniversary party. I don't know why I threw them in my overnight bag —I just did—and now I know why!" I said with even more excitement, and I just couldn't come down off of it. I was officially Jeff's girlfriend, and I couldn't be happier.

"Let's get our first boyfriend/girlfriend picture together," he said.

"Yes, let's do that!"

We laughed as we sat back on the couch as he put his right arm around me and I cuddled up to him while I had my right arm wrapped around him. He extended his arm out as his phone pointed to us and took the picture. He wrote something in regard to me being his girlfriend. He really wanted the world to know.

"Ready?" he asked me with a smile.

"Ready," I replied.

He posted the picture to all of his social media pages, and it only took seconds for the flood of likes and comments to start coming in . . . as well as other opinions.

CHAPTER THIRTEEN

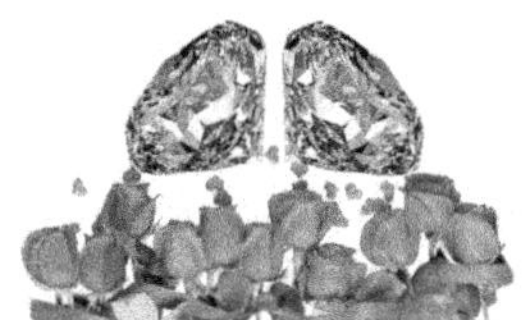

"Karis, I wouldn't be so upset about this. He's clearly trying to make you mad by claiming that he made Liz his girlfriend. I just can't believe he's being a hundred percent honest about this," Beverly said, as they sat in the family room of Karis's house.

"I agree with Beverly," Chloe said. "He's just doing this to get under your skin. You know how Jeff is. So who cares if he bought her a brand-new Porsche Panamera, some Jimmy Choo's, an Oscar de la Renta dress, and a Judith Leiber bag? It means nothing, Karis, and you know that."

"Don't forget the two-hundred roses at the concert the day he met her. Buying a woman he didn't even know that many roses? That was damn insane!" Beverly said as she shook her head and then took a sip of her drink.

"I know it means nothing, you two. But he's never bought me a car," Karis replied, as she breastfed her nine-month-old daughter.

"He may have never bought you a car, Karis, but he bought you an alligator Hermes Birkin bag that's the price of one," Beverly reminded her.

Karis shook her head. "I don't understand why he's doing this to me. He knew I wanted to get back together with him and he has the audacity to throw another woman all up in my face, buys her all of this expensive stuff, and then makes her his girlfriend. He hasn't even been knowing her for that long. I knew him much longer than she did before he made me his girlfriend."

"And that's just it, Karis, she's just his girlfriend. He can break up with her tomorrow even though he just asked her today. Nothing is definite. I think it's a great time now more than ever to try and get him back. There is no other man like Jeff Vick out there that is single, and when I say single, I mean not married. He's one of a kind, and he deserves you and he deep down inside knows it," Chloe said.

"He absolutely deserves you, Karis. That Liz chick doesn't fit in anyone's circles. She's an outsider. She's just someone that's on his rebound list and once he bounces back to reality he will see that it was meant to be between the two of you all along. But now, there's a lot at stake, and you got Jenelle's ass always trying to ruin things between the two of you as well," Beverly said.

"I can't stand her, but it's not her I want back because I'm not gay, it's Jeff," Karis declared, and then kissed her daughter on the forehead.

"Then you need to do whatever you can to get him back, Karis. He doesn't belong with Liz, he belongs with *you,*" Beverly stressed, as Chloe nodded with a smile in agreement.

Jeff pulled up in his Bugatti to the valet area in front of an expensive steak and seafood restaurant, somewhere I'd never been to before, but was very curious about trying the food. All eyes were on us as we waited for a valet attendant to walk over to his car, and I noticed that people had their phones up, obviously getting pictures of Jeff's car.

We walked towards the front entrance holding hands as people took pictures of us and some even shouted questions at us.

"Jeff and Liz, is this your first date as a couple?" a woman asked as she stuck her phone out to us as if it was a microphone.

Should've known some of the media showed up here.

"Yes, it is. And my girlfriend and I plan on having a nice and quiet dinner tonight. Thank you," Jeff said with a smile as two employees held the doors open for us.

"I love your bag and shoes, Liz," a woman said.

"Thank you," I said with a surprised smile. I didn't know why I wasn't expecting compliments, but I really wasn't. I felt that everything had changed for me once I'd met Jeff, but it was now on another level since we were officially a couple. I knew that our privacy was always gonna be in question and that going out anywhere—with or without him—I was taking my chances of always having my privacy invaded. I guess this was what I had to live with by being the girlfriend of a billionaire. I wasn't used to this at all, and never knew if I ever would be.

"So," Jeff said with a smile as he looked at his menu. "What looks good?"

"Everything," I replied as I looked at my menu as well.

He laughed. "Order anything you want."

After ordering anything I wanted, we got a good conversation going.

"So, as my new girlfriend, I'm giving you the option on whether you wanna keep working or not?"

I looked at him as if I couldn't believe what he'd asked me, but he was for real. "Oh, wow. I didn't expect to hear this." I sighed. "I can honestly say that I'm burnt out on working there already and I've only been there for seven years. I don't see any advancement in a place like that. The people who are at the top are not leaving anytime soon, and not only that, they always hire people that they already know for the better positions. I guess I'm not that desperate to wanna do anything just to get ahead and if I wanted to get ahead which I always did, I was gonna go to a different company and do it by working hard."

"I know what you mean, Liz. So that's why I'm giving you this option. You know no matter what I'll always take care of you."

"I'll put my notice in tonight," I declared.

He laughed. "That was fast!"

"Hey, how many chances am I gonna get to quit my job when I get a new boyfriend? None of my past boyfriends never ever offered me that option. Most women quit their jobs when they get engaged and especially after getting married. It's very rare for a woman to quit it when she gets a new boyfriend, but you're no ordinary boyfriend."

"Yeah, I admit that I'm not. I just like to know that I can see you at any time. We can go places and I don't have to worry about you being so stressed about work you don't have to do."

"Wow, Jeff. You can make a woman get really used to your lifestyle very fast, huh?"

He grinned. "Well, I haven't had too many girlfriends and as you know I've never been married; not even engaged. I just know when something feels right, and when it doesn't, well, then I know the relationship is not gonna last. I'm not perfect when it comes to relationships otherwise I feel I would've been married by now."

"Well, you have no problem getting any woman, obviously, but it's all about knowing who's right for you."

"And now I know," he said with a smile.

"Um, Jeff?"

"What's up, baby?" he asked, and took a sip of his non-alcoholic drink.

"You know, giving a woman so much so fast can make her feel, you know, entitled."

He looked at me. "Do you feel entitled now?"

"No," I honestly replied. "I know I'm not owed a fairytale lifestyle, but I can see how easily a woman can get hooked on living this way."

"That's why I never married any of my past girlfriends because that's exactly how they felt—entitled. Just because I can give a woman anything she wants doesn't mean I'm going to so she shouldn't expect it even though I know she always does. You would think that would be common sense but it's not for most of them."

"You're right, it isn't." My phone rang. It was Laurel. "Laurel."

He grinned once again. "Aren't you gonna answer it?"

"Nope. I don't feel like talking to her right now because I know what she's calling me about."

"Yeah, I have a feeling, too," he said as his grin was bigger. "But you'll eventually talk to her."

"Yeah, but not right now. I'm the happiest I've been in years and we're having a great conversation." I turned my phone completely off because I didn't want her calling or texting me. Because of what I'd overheard her say, I felt that she didn't think he would ask me to be his girlfriend and this soon at that, and now she wanted to act as if she didn't say those things, but I would remind her of it when I was ready.

"I'm glad to hear that you're the happiest you've been in years. That means a lot to me. When I meet someone and fall for her like the way I fell for you, that's all I wanna do is make her happy. I had no idea what your situation was like when we first met, so I'm glad I've made it better."

"Yeah, you most definitely have. I mean, I wasn't in dire straits or severely depressed or anything, but I can't say that I was always happy. I suffered from depression for a while after my breakup with Devin, but we're not here to talk about that. It's a new beginning for me and that's all I wanna focus on."

"I definitely agree with that."

We kissed.

The waiter came to our table and put two orders of jumbo shrimp cocktail in front of us along with a cocktail sauce that was so loud I could use it to clear my sinuses without even getting that close to it.

"Whew! This sauce!" I said, and slowly dipped one of my shrimp into it. "Never had a sauce this hot, spicy and tangy before."

"Yeah, this restaurant is known for it," Jeff said with a laugh, and dove right into his as if it was something he ate all the time when he was here. "It's delicious to me."

"And to me as well," I said as my eyes watered from eating it.

He looked at his phone. "Excuse me," he said, and got up and left the table.

Here we go again . . . and again.

But I felt it was different this time. I was officially his girlfriend. I now had the right to know why he was getting calls and getting up and walking off from me once he had. I looked at my phone and turned it back on, and it instantly rang.

Laurel, again.

"Laurel. What do you want?" I asked.

"Why are you sounding all like that, Liz? You should be the happiest woman in this world right now," she said.

"Well, no one is the happiest in the world. I felt that way for several minutes after he'd asked me to be his girlfriend, but now it happened again."

"Uh, oh!" she said. "He ran off after getting a call, right?"

"Yeah, right," I said as I rolled my eyes. I looked around for Jeff and I didn't see him anywhere in sight. "Honestly, Laurel, I don't know if it's still any of my business because he just made me his girlfriend and I feel that I only became his girlfriend because I wasn't being a nagging bitch by always asking him who he was talking to because to be honest it was none of my business."

"But you're his girlfriend now, Liz. You're on a whole other level. He asked you so that means he's serious about you. Yeah, you might wanna still not ask him because he just made you his girlfriend, but if he keeps this up then you might just wanna casually mention it to him. You never know, he's probably wondering why you haven't mentioned it to him yet."

"But that's just it, he probably likes the fact that I'm not all up in his business asking him all of these questions every time his phone rings and he runs off. That's probably one of things that he likes about me and probably one of the many reasons why he made me his girlfriend. I just wanna keep doing the right things, Laurel. This relationship is way too important to me to mess it up because I'm always nagging him every single time he gets a phone call or text."

"Yeah, I agree. Just play it safe for right now. It's clear that you're doing everything right and that's why he made you his girlfriend and so fast at that."

"And he also said I could quit my job," I informed her.

"What?!" she shrieked. "Are you serious, Liz? Are you going to?"

"Of course. I'm putting my notice in tonight. He said he will take care of me. How many chances am I gonna get at being with someone like Jeff? He said he doesn't want me stressing about work I don't have to do and I have to agree with him."

"Wow, Liz. He really, really likes you. I have to admit that I'm very envious of all of this already."

It's about time you said it, I thought. "But that's just it. I don't want you or anyone being envious of me being his girlfriend now because it's clear he's hiding something from me that he really doesn't want me to know about and I have to find out what the hell it is, otherwise I just don't think I'm gonna be fully happy in this relationship."

"Yeah, you definitely need to find out what's up with why he's always running off when he gets a call when you're around. Maybe slowly bring it up to him—but not right now—or maybe one day he will just tell you if you just casually ask."

"Yeah, maybe," I said, as Jeff made his way back to the table as women stared at him with a smile, but his smile and eyes were all on me. "Jeff's coming back to the table, gotta go."

"Okay."

He sat back down. "Who was that?"

"Laurel," I replied with a grin.

He returned the grin. "So, I see the two of you are already back on speaking terms, huh?"

"Yeah. I'm still a little upset about what I overheard her say to our mom and the way she treated Marlon because she thought my new car was hers, but I knew she was gonna keep calling. I knew she was gonna start as soon as she found out through social media that you asked me to be your girlfriend. She said she's envious, of course, but she really shouldn't be."

"No, she shouldn't be, I agree. She's got a great husband and daughter."

"She does. I also told her how you don't want me to work. I think she's truly jealous about that and even said so."

He laughed. "Well, I always give my new girlfriend that option about whether or not she still wants to work. All of them quit their jobs, but as you see it didn't work out with any of them so some had to start working again and some found other men they could leech off of, but I wasn't the one anymore to do that to. I don't like entitled women, but then again I am to blame for it when they get too comfortable."

I nodded with a smile as I ate some more of my shrimp cocktail as I now wondered how comfortable in this relationship should I really get because it was not guaranteed that I was gonna be with him long term. And I think in a lot of ways he wanted me to know that without actually telling me, and believe me, I got the point . . . faster than he asked me to be his girlfriend.

CHAPTER FOURTEEN

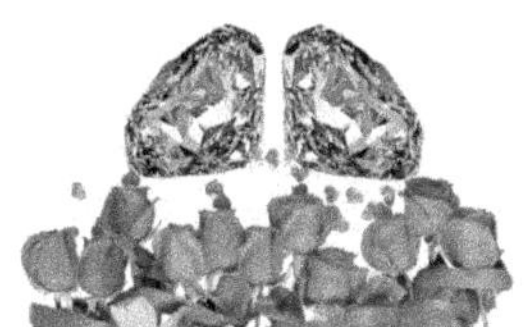

"One . . . Two . . . THREE!" Jeff and I said, and laughed as we ran and jumped into his private pool at his private luxury villa in Maldives.

We laughed as we splashed each other with water, and I swam to the edge of the pool to take in this majestic view.

"Wow, this is really beautiful. I swear it doesn't even look real," I said. "I can't believe I'm here. I could be at work right now—bored as hell doing repetitive work while busting my ass and getting absolutely nowhere—but I'm in my boyfriend's private pool at his private villa in freakin' Maldives! One of the prettiest places in the world. If I'm dreaming, like I said a million times, please don't wake me up."

He laughed as he held me. "You're not dreaming, Liz. I'm glad you don't take anything for granted unlike what my ex-girlfriends did, but I'm not here to talk about them."

"Yeah, but they're talking a lot on social media about our new relationship, especially that Karis and her friends. I wish people would just stay out of our business. We're together now so they need to move on, especially her."

He grinned. "Yeah, especially her. She's the worst one of them all."

"Yeah, I can tell," I said, as he continued to hold me as I still took in the view. I faced him. "You know, it's amazing how I wasn't even gonna go to that concert that night—I can't help but to think about it —and look where it's led?"

"Something was telling you to go so you went. I was waiting for you and I didn't even know it myself."

We kissed.

"Um, what would've happened if I didn't show, you know? Would you have given those roses to another woman?"

"I would've saved a lot of money that night," he said with an even bigger grin.

I blushed. "So I was *the only one* you felt was worth giving two-hundred roses to?"

"Absolutely," he replied with a smile. "And since we've gotten to this point, I was right to do what I did."

We kissed once again.

"So, since we're officially a couple, is there something you wanna tell me?"

I had to ask. I wanted to see if he would come out and say it, but I wasn't sure if he knew what I was talking about.

He gave me a confused look. "Tell you what, Liz?"

I shrugged. "Anything. Anything that's been bothering you; I don't know."

His look of confusion now turned into a look of suspicion. "I think you do know, Liz. What is it that you wanna know about me?"

I didn't know if this was gonna upset him or not, and I didn't wanna take the chance if I knew it was going to, but I had a reason to wanna know things now that I was his girlfriend. "Um, how you made your billions?" I decided to ask.

He chuckled. "I thought you already knew. I thought I told you."

"No, you never did," I honestly replied.

"So you think how I made my billions is bothering me? Or is it bothering you?" he asked with a slight grin.

I sighed. I didn't wanna go around in a circle of confusion. "No, Jeff. I just wanted to know in general was anything bothering you, that's all."

"I'm as fine as a great wine. And you?"

"Things can't get much better for me, I know that much. I'm the luckiest woman in the world right now." And if I wanted to stay that way, I knew I needed to not be so nosey and just enjoy my time with my new billionaire boyfriend.

Billionaire boyfriend.

How many women in this world could say their boyfriend was a billionaire and a black one at that?

"You still wanna know how I made my billions?"

"Of course," I said with a smile.

"Investing. My parents opened up an investment account for my sister and me when we were first born. We wanted the money to stay in and grow and grow, and only sold stocks when our broker advised us to do it. Well, a lot of the stocks shot through the roof—20,000% up and more—and those were the ones we had the most money invested in, and it's when I was making a lot of money being a neurosurgeon. I hardly spent the money I made in my career on anything, and put most of it in investments, and as you see it paid off big time for me where I was able to retire early and live the life I always wanted to live."

"Incredible. But it's like anyone can live like this if they did what you and your family did. But your life wasn't all that bad being a neurosurgeon."

"Absolutely not, and I was able to attract a lot of women in my profession, but it's something about being at billionaire status. There's nothing else like it, no matter what color you are."

"Very true, Jeff. And I'm glad you wanna share your lifestyle with me."

"Glad to have you a part of it." He got out of the water. "Gotta get something. I'll be right back."

I watched as he looked at his phone that was sitting on the lounge chair . . . and put it back down and went inside the villa.

I stared at the phone. I was tempted to see if there were any texts on it that he didn't want me to see. I got out of the water and toweled myself off while I stared in great curiosity at his phone. I was his girlfriend now and felt that there was a lot he still wasn't telling me, and I felt that I gave him that chance. I also believed—I didn't know what it was—that he knew I was asking about those texts he'd received and left my presence when he did.

I got up off of my chair and looked at his phone. I tapped it and saw a picture of him and me that was taken on his private jet on the way here. I smiled. I jumped by the chime that was coming from not his phone, but mine. I picked it up and looked at it:

Your relationship with Jeff will NOT LAST!!!!!!

"Just who the fuck is this?!"

"What?" Jeff asked with a grin as he held a bag in his hands. "Who are you talking to?"

"This text I just received!" I angrily replied and showed it to him.

He looked at it and shook his head. "Just a hater, Liz. You know what to do. Ignore it and block them."

"How the hell did this person get my number?! I don't give my number out to random people!"

"Who knows, Liz. Look, don't let this ruin your time here, okay? I took you here so we can get away from everything and have some real fun together since we're officially together."

I smiled. "Yeah, you're right, Jeff. I should've known that being with someone like you that it was gonna bring out all sorts of haters, that's a fact. I guess it's just something that I have to get used to since I've never had a billionaire boyfriend. I mean, no one cared that I was with Devin all of those years."

"Yeah, it's different, Liz. A lot of people acted very nasty towards my girlfriends at the time. I wish there was something I could do about it, but it just comes with the territory when you're with a man of my status; not trying to sound or be arrogant at all, but it's true."

"Yeah, you're right, it's the truth, Jeff. Nothing arrogant about the truth."

He nodded with a smile. "Well, let's cheer you up, shall we?" He handed me the bag. "For you."

"I feel better already!" I said with excitement before I saw what was in the bag.

He laughed as he waited for me to open my latest gift from him, but I didn't wanna only feel good when he gave me a gift because even though he could afford to buy me anything, I just felt there was an ulterior motive behind it, I just couldn't prove it, and why did I even wanna try? *I* was his girlfriend, not any other woman, and I felt like the luckiest and most spoiled woman in the world.

"Here, open this one first," he said, as he gave me the box.

Van Cleef and Arpels.

Good Lord!

"Goodness, I *love* this brand! I don't have any pieces from it," I said, as I slowly took the ribbon off of the box.

"Now your collection has just started," he said with a smile.

I popped open the box and shrieked in shock. "Jeff! Oh, my God! This is BEAUTIFUL!" I said, and could hear my voice echo throughout the area since we were the only villa in this area. I was reacting to a beautiful ring called the Between the Finger ring made with white gold that had two butterflies covered in diamonds. Just stunning.

"Here, let me put it on your right-hand fingers," he said, and slipped the ring on where the butterflies rested on my middle and ring fingers.

I couldn't stop staring at it. "I am at a loss for words. I wanted something from this brand so bad but couldn't even afford their least expensive piece."

He nodded with a smile. "Yeah, this brand is very pricey; been around for a very long time. I'm glad I'm able to get you something from it."

"And never did I think in a million years that this would be my first-ever piece, though! How much was this?"

"$27,900," he replied as if it was $27.90.

"Wow," I said as I still stared at it. "You really spoil me, Jeff. I don't think I'll ever be able to thank you enough for all of the gifts you've given me, starting with those two-hundred roses when we first met."

"What else is money for?" he said with a huge grin. "I got too much of it so I love to give it to people and spend it on people who appreciate it."

"And I appreciate it, Jeff, very much."

He gave me the last box.

"Oh, Lord!" I said again when I saw the name on the box.

Rolex.

"I had a fake Rolex when I was in high school," I confessed with a grin. "I tried to pretend it was real, but no one believed me and actually laughed at me and said I insulted their intelligence—I did. I think it was because you could see that another brand was erased on the dial and 'Rolex' was stamped over it."

He burst into laughter! "Yeah, an obvious fake! That'll do it! But this one is real, no questions about it."

"I'll never question authenticity with anything you buy me because I simply don't have to," I replied with a smile as I opened the box . . . and almost passed out.

In this box was one of the most beautiful watches I'd ever seen. I was speechless.

He chuckled because he knew I was truly at a loss for words. "It's the Lady Datejust Oyster 31-millimeter, yellow gold with diamonds and mother-of-pearl butterflies in the face of it."

I just kept staring at it. I thought the ring was beautiful, and now he gives me this out-of-this-world Rolex watch that looked as if it came with it.

"Are you okay?" he asked with a grin.

I jumped all over him and smothered him with kisses; he laughed hard. "I can't thank you enough for this, Jeff. This is by far the most beautiful watch I've ever owned. Ever. Far from the fake I had in high school that I got embarrassed about showing off. But I can't show this one off; it's too beautiful and expensive. People will just have to see it when I wear it."

"How about wearing it now?" he suggested.

"Something wrong with my first edition Apple watch with its dirty white straps?"

He laughed hard once again. "Nothing at all. As you see, I'm wearing the latest Apple watch. I'm a watch guy as well as a shoe guy. Just wanted my girlfriend to have a beautiful watch as well."

I took off my Apple watch. "Hook it on, baby!"

He laughed as he hooked the Rolex on my wrist and the diamonds danced under the warmth of the afternoon sun as the yellow gold strap and mother of pearl butterflies did as well. It was so beautiful it didn't even look real as I slowly turned my wrist as I couldn't stop looking at it.

"So, how much?" I asked.

He laughed once again.

I laughed as well. "That much, huh?"

"$55,400," he said with a smile, but once again said it like it was $55.40.

"No comment," I said as I kept staring at the watch. "More than a car and what most people make a year right here on my wrist."

He laughed once again. "True, and I'm glad you don't take anything for granted, Liz."

"Absolutely not."

"Come here," he said, as he sat back on the chair. "Sit in front of me."

I did what he said as he held me as he continued to sit behind me. I continued to stare at this watch, and then looked at my right hand and at the beautiful ring that was on it. I didn't take a damn thing for granted since I was officially a billionaire's girlfriend and I was in pure bliss, and I didn't want anyone to ruin it. But I couldn't get it out of my mind that there were people who were hellbent on ruining it, but I had to admit this was what I had to put up with now. I was in a whole different lifestyle on a whole other level, so all of this came with the territory.

CHAPTER FIFTEEN

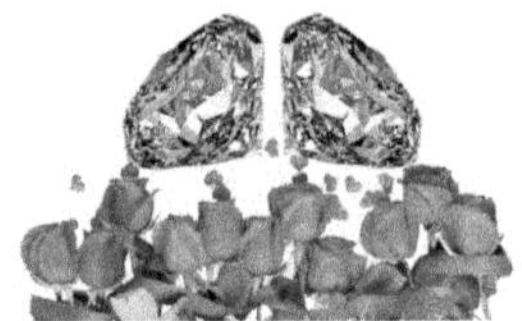

Fresh popcorn, sweet and sugary candy and soda, and a new movie was on the agenda tonight for the monthly Auntie and Niece Night, a special time of the month that both my beautiful niece Autumn and I always looked forward to and was held each time Laurel and Marlon went out on their monthly date. I told her I would never stop having these with her no matter what.

We settled in her bedroom on her bed in front of her 4K TV in our pajamas armed with our goodies, but Autumn also had two of my goodies—my Judith Leiber crystal red rose bag and my Jimmy Choo crystal red shoes. She loved them so much she said she wanted to have them in bed with her while we watched the movie for tonight. She even had me take pictures of her earlier in my shoes that looked gigantic on her little feet while the bag hung very low on her shoulder and was practically touching the floor. But she looked too cute so I didn't mind doing it at all and her parents and grandparents loved it when we texted them pictures of it.

"You have better things than Mommy, Aunt Lizzie," she said with a smile.

"Don't tell your mom that," I said with a grin as I tried not to laugh. "Your mom has a lot of nice things as well from your dad and what she buys for herself, so she shouldn't complain."

"And she complains a lot since you've been with Jeff."

I grinned. "I know she has, honey. And I'm sorry you have to hear it and your dad has to hear it as well."

She looked at me with her beautiful dark brown eyes. "Is she jealous of you?"

I wanted to laugh. She was so innocent in everything, but even she knew how her mom was treating me since the gifts from Jeff had gotten bigger and were gonna get even bigger since I was officially his girlfriend. "I don't think so, baby. She has nothing to be jealous of. Jeff is just my boyfriend. He just happens to have a lot of money."

"He has a *gazillion* dollars!" she said with a big smile.

I laughed. "He has a lot of money, baby, and it does seem like a gazillion dollars. But above all, he's a very nice and respectable man."

"I don't like boys yet—eeeewwww! But when I do, I want a man like my dad or Jeff because you've been so happy since being with him, Aunt Lizzie."

I smiled and kissed her on her forehead. "That's good to hear, honey. And yes, I've been very happy with Jeff. And never settle for just anyone. You have so much time so you don't have to worry about boys right now and not for several, several years, okay?"

"Don't worry, Aunt Lizzie, I know and I don't."

"Great, baby. So, are you ready to watch *Cruella*?"

"YES!" she said with full-fledged excitement.

"Okay," I laughed, and turned on the movie.

Here was an six-year-old girl who was already talking about wanting a man like Jeff because she'd seen how happy I was since being with him. I didn't wanna tell her that it wasn't all what she thought it was because she was way too young for that kind of conversation, but if she ever met a man like Jeff, she would definitely see it for herself.

Several minutes into the movie, I received a text:

Do you know where your man is?

I looked at Autumn and she was already very much into the movie so I didn't wanna pause it or anything, and I didn't wanna have go back and forth with this person because once again, I had no idea who this was, so I print-screened the text and saved it. I wanted to build a case.

CHAPTER SIXTEEN

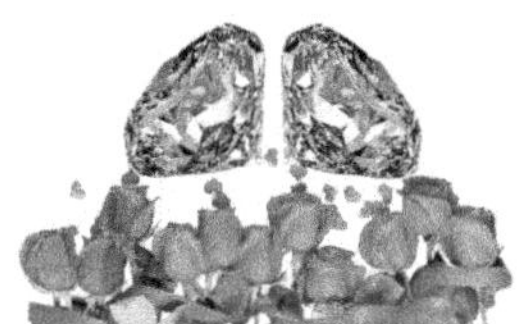

"Thanks for taking me on one of the best shopping sprees I've ever been on, Jenelle. I really appreciate it," I said, as we walked to a restaurant of my choice, which Jenelle was paying for.

"No problem, Liz. I must say that I never went anywhere with Karis; can't stand her and I mean it," she said, as she walked proudly head-to-toe in Balmain while wearing a beautiful, huge Afro wig. "You're truly special to Jeff."

"And that's so great to hear. I just can't believe I'm his girlfriend. I never thought I would be this happy so soon in my life after my breakup with my last boyfriend."

"Yeah, breakups are hard. Believe me, it's no different no matter what your sexual preference is. I've been through so many relationships with women I just don't know if I'll ever find true happiness like what you found with my brother."

"You will, Jenelle. Just like your brother, you can have any woman you want. You're beautiful and intelligent."

"Thanks, Liz," she said, and winked at me. She laughed at my surprise reaction. "Don't worry, Liz. I'm not trying to hit on you. I know my limits."

"It's okay, really. I just would've never thought."

She laughed again. "Yeah, a lot don't think I am, but it's okay because I am who I am."

I sighed as we continued to walk to the restaurant.

She looked at me. "What is it, Liz?"

"I know I shouldn't bring this up, but I'm tired of this happening. And just to let you know, I haven't mentioned this to Jeff."

"Uh, oh. What's going on?"

I pulled my phone out of my purse and showed her the saved texts.

She looked at them and shook her head. "Looks like Karis and I are gonna have to have a nice little chit chat. I'm not gonna have her and her little cronies harassing you since you're my brother's new girlfriend."

"You really think it's her?"

"Who else could it be?"

I shrugged. "I really don't know. I know I shouldn't assume that it's her or one of her friends because I really have no proof. And I didn't wanna keep bugging and whining to Jeff about them."

"But have you talked to him about them?"

"Yeah, I have, but it was only about the first text that I'd received when we were in Maldives. I just want this to stop. I feel like someone is watching my every move with him," I said, and took a quick look around me.

She grinned. "I think whosever doing this to you is nowhere near here, Liz. Look, Jeff is a black billionaire. The rarest of the rare. He can have any woman he wants and he wanted you so he made you his girlfriend. Jeff doesn't make just any woman his girlfriend, Liz, and I think you know that by now."

"Yeah, I know and I still can't believe it. And I'm just his girlfriend, though, and I'm being harassed like this by some hater."

"And that's exactly what this person is—a hater, Liz. I'm not sure if this is really Karis or not, but it's pretty hard for me *not* to believe it's her."

"What are you gonna do?"

"I'll talk to her about it whether she wants to or not. I think she's scared of me."

I laughed. "Yeah, I got that impression of her, too!"

We reached the restaurant and walked into it . . . .

And I immediately noticed Karis and her friends Beverly and Chloe!

"Jenelle! They're here! I don't believe this!" I whispered.

"I see," she replied with a smirk. "You can't make this shit up, Liz, you really can't. I don't think this is any coincidence at all since I posted on social media that we were going shopping and were coming here for lunch, and I know all of those cunts secretly follow me but still openly follow Jeff. Get ready, because this is gonna be the most interesting lunch at a restaurant you're ever gonna have."

I started to get nervous. I didn't want her causing a scene especially since this was all about me and something that I couldn't prove. But we were here and so were they and I had to agree with Jenelle, I didn't believe for one second that it was a coincidence. I was just starting to get to know Jenelle so I had no idea what she was capable of.

We were seated at our reserved table as Jenelle's eyes stayed glue to Karis and her friends since we were in direct view of their table. I noticed how Karis had her baby with her and I saw just how real the situation was between her and Jeff and why he wasn't with her anymore.

"What are you gonna do?" I asked, as we looked at our menus.

"I'm just gonna talk to her, that's all. No need to cause a scene. I just need your phone for proof that she's been sending the messages."

"But I'm not so sure if it's her, Jenelle."

"If it's her—which I think it is—she's gonna have to admit it today and she's not leaving here until she does. If she doesn't try and start shit then I won't start any. And she would be a fool to start anything considering the fact she has her baby with her; and she wonders why my brother doesn't wanna have anything to do with her anymore. He saw her for the whore she really is."

"Yeah, that's what he told me," I replied. I changed the subject. "Wow, there are no prices on this menu. That makes me nervous."

"Not me," she said with a grin.

"That's because you're from a billionaire family, Jenelle. And I think you and your parents are some of the nicest people I've ever met, especially for someone of y'alls status."

She smiled. "Thank you, Liz. I knew my brother knew a good woman when he saw you at the concert that night. He called me the day after and told me he thinks he met his next girlfriend."

"For real, Jenelle?" I asked as I smiled big.

"Yeah, he said that. You know I'll never lie to you about anything." She shot Karis a quick glare. "And she better not either."

"I hope not as well, but I don't wanna cause any trouble."

"No trouble at all. I just want her to confess to all of this fuckery because I believe that it's her, Liz. She'll do anything to get Jeff back. The only person she's fooling about thinking that she's getting him back is herself."

"I really like Jeff. I'm just his girlfriend and he's the best boyfriend I've ever had, and I'm not just saying that because he's a billionaire. I just never thought I would ever be in a relationship like this and I just don't want anyone trying to ruin it for me because they can't accept us being together and just don't know how to move on."

"Well, she's gonna move on today, guaranteed."

I smiled, but didn't want anything to get out of control because at this point I just didn't know what was gonna happen. I looked at my phone. It was Jeff. "It's Jeff."

"Good, ask him how did the shareholders meeting go."

I nodded with a smile. "Hey, honey."

"Hey, baby. The meeting ended early. Are you still shopping with Jenelle?"

"No, we're actually having lunch right now."

"Tell him who's here," Jenelle said with a grin.

I didn't wanna start any drama, but I felt he had to know. I sighed. "Jenelle wanted me to let you know that your ex and her friends are here at this restaurant."

"What restaurant?"

I told him the name of it.

"I'm not far from there. See you soon."

"He's on his way," I informed Jenelle.

"Good, because there's nothing like him confronting her as well. It'll stick more with him telling her than with me telling her."

Minutes later, Jeff walked in. We locked eyes as we smiled at each other. More than half of the women in the restaurant were looking at him. He was dressier more than usual since he had the meeting and looked absolutely gorgeous. I still couldn't believe he was my boyfriend.

He passed Karis, Beverly, and Chloe, and nodded to them in acknowledgment.

I stood up as he approached our table.

"Hey, baby" he said to me.

We kissed.

"Hey, sis," he said, and gave her a kiss on the cheek.

"Hey, bro," she said with a smile. "Glad you made it. Now you can pay for this lunch."

"No problem," he said with a laugh.

I looked over at Karis and locked eyes with her. I honestly thought she hated me. She was acting as if I'd stolen Jeff from her. "Have you ever been here before?" I asked Jeff.

"Many times," he said, as he looked at the menu. "But this is very special since I'm with you as well as with my sister. We don't have too many lunches like this anymore."

"We sure don't," Jenelle said with a smile. "So, is everyone ready to order? Because I'm getting hungry," she said, as she glared over at Karis.

Jeff grinned. "Stay cool, sis. We'll talk to them when we leave."

Lunch was over.

And it went way faster than I thought it would.

Karis and her friends were still here, and since they were here before we all got here, it was clear that they weren't leaving until we did.

I felt as if they were stalking Jeff and me.

"Let's go," Jeff said with a smile.

We all got up from the table, and Jenelle headed straight towards Karis's table!

"Oh, my God! She's really gonna do it!" I said to Jeff.

"Well, it's either now or never," he replied as if this was no big deal at all.

But I found it to be a very big deal. I didn't like what was going on in our relationship already with these anonymous texts from a jealous, scorned woman who obviously couldn't let go of the fact that Jeff had moved on from her and now was with me. I wanted this to end once and for all, and now I had all the reason in the world to believe that this was Karis all along.

We all stopped by their table as they all looked up at us as if they didn't know why we were standing here.

"What?" Karis asked.

"You know *what,* Karis. Don't play dumb," Jenelle said.

Karis looked at Jeff. "What is she talking about?"

Jeff sighed. "Look, I don't wanna make a scene, especially since we're all in public. I just have one thing to ask you, Karis."

"What is it?" Karis asked, as her baby slept in her stroller.

"And before he asks her this, the two of you better not interrupt in anything that we're asking," Jenelle warned Beverly and Chloe.

They looked at each other and then turned their attention back to Jeff.

"Are you the person sending these anonymous texts to Liz?" he asked Karis, and showed her my phone.

She looked at them as Beverly and Chloe tried to look over at them as Jeff held my phone right in front of her face. She sighed. "I'm only gonna say this once. *No*. I haven't. Why would I do some childish shit like that, Jeff? You know me."

"Damn right he knows you," Jenelle said.

"Your brother is talking to me," Karis informed her.

"Now, bitch, don't get smart! I don't care if you have your kid here with you and you're sitting here with your only two friends. He was asking you a question!"

"And I answered him," Karis replied. "I'm not gonna argue about something I didn't do, and I don't know who's doing it, but it's not me."

I looked at Jenelle as she shook her head. I could tell she really didn't believe her.

"Why should we believe you, Karis? You've wanted Jeff back since he broke up with you and now you're mad because he's with Liz," Jenelle said.

"Okay, okay. We're not gonna get into all of this here. All I'm gonna say is you better not be lying about it not being you, Karis, and I mean it," Jeff warned her.

"I have nothing else to say about it," Karis informed him.

I looked at my phone . . . .

Do you really believe Jeff was at a shareholders meeting? How dumb can you be?

I gasped. I tried to control my breathing. "Ummm, guys?" I said to Jeff and Jenelle.

"What is it?" Jeff asked.

"Yeah, what's up, Liz?" Jenelle said.

I took a deep breath. "It's not her."

CHAPTER SEVENTEEN

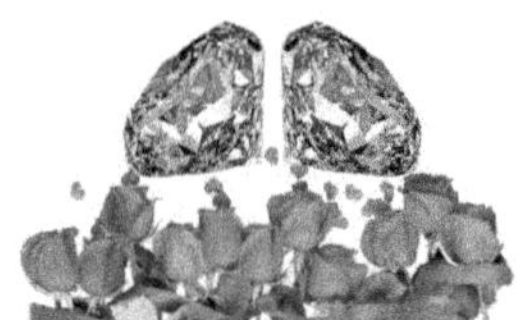

"Liz, I really was at the shareholders meeting this afternoon. Whoever is really doing this is really trying to ruin our relationship and I don't want that to happen. Do you?"

"Of course not, Jeff. This is the best relationship I've been in and I'm not just saying this because of the lifestyle and everything. You've been so good to me since the first day we met. I just didn't think I would find happiness this fast again, and never in my wildest dreams did I ever think I would have a billionaire boyfriend. Things like this don't happen to women every day, and it's clear that someone wants to sabotage what we've built in our relationship so far."

"Well, only we can make sure that someone doesn't sabotage it and we keep building on what we've got because we've got something good, Liz, very good," he said, as we sat in the recreation room of his house after lunch. "Damn, that text could not have come at a better time. I mean, what are the odds of that happening where I'm confronting Karis about it and a text comes into your phone? Now that was proof it isn't her, right?"

"Exactly right. I hate to say this, but it took something like that to happen for me to officially believe it was not her, Jeff, I can't lie. If that didn't happen then I think I'll still be convinced that it was her, and I know Jenelle would be as well."

"I know, and so would Karis."

I looked at him. "What about you?"

He shrugged. "It's possible it could've very well been Karis, but I admit I've had a lot of flings with women, more than having girlfriends. I've only given very few women my number, though."

"Oh, yeah? But how did they get mine? This is *me* they're fucking with, not you! Now that we know it's not Karis, is there someone else out there that you haven't told me about?"

He grinned. "Look, Liz, like I said, I've been with a lot of women, but very few have made it to girlfriend status like the way you and Karis did. I honestly can't narrow it down. And I'm sorry someone got your number. That's the last thing I wanted to happen, but you know you can always change it."

"No, I'm not gonna do that because I wanna know who this person is so I can tell them to their face to leave me the fuck alone. I didn't do anything to anyone. It's clear that it has to be someone who wants you and wants you bad."

"Or it can be someone who wants you and wants you bad . . . or back."

I looked at him. "Huh?"

"Liz. How do you know a woman is doing this? We just eliminated the most obvious woman, and you saw proof right in front of her and all of us that it wasn't her. I just couldn't get myself to be a hundred percent convinced of it, either, and the only reason why I couldn't is because I believe she is trying to get me back and wouldn't do something like that because she knows if she did then I would never speak to her again."

"You don't still have feelings for her, do you?"

"Absolutely not, Liz. If I did, I would've never made you my girlfriend."

I smiled. "Well, that's good to hear. But I still need to find out who's doing this because I feel that I can never be fully happy until I do."

"I wouldn't worry about it. All I want us to do is build on our relationship more and more each day; I sound like a song, huh?"

I laughed. "Yeah, you do!"

We kissed.

"You know, it's been a long time since I've been this happy as well, and I want things to stay this way between us. Anonymous texts and stalking and all kinds of shit can ruin the best of relationships. I may have the billionaire lifestyle, but it's nothing if I can't enjoy it with someone who's special to me, but I'm not naïve in the fact that I know we'll never be problem-free."

I was truly flattered. "And you're special to me as well. And you're right, no relationship is problem-free."

And I wanted to keep on being special to him, but I had so many unanswered questions. I hooked my arm in his and laid my head on his shoulder as we watched TV.

His phone lit up in silence. He looked at it. "Be right back."

I nodded with a fake smile.

It was happening again, and it was gonna keep happening. I needed to know who the hell this was that kept calling him where he had to get up and answer it in private. I wasn't holding back anymore, I was gonna find out once and for all.

CHAPTER EIGHTEEN

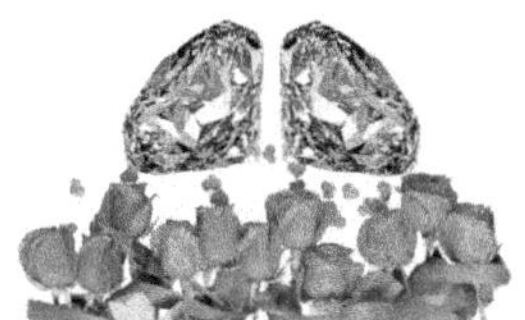

"I just can't believe it's not Karis! I just can't believe it!" I said, as I paced briskly back and forth in front of Laurel and Marlon as they sat on the couch in the family room. "This is nuts! I have no idea who it can be now."

"Well, I personally wouldn't care who it is, Liz. I think you're thinking way too much about this. You don't have the kind of boyfriend most women have—hell, most women don't have the kind of husband that you have as a boyfriend. It's clear that when you're with someone like Jeff there's always gonna be some woman out there who thinks she should be with him instead of you and will try to do anything to ruin your relationship with him."

"And that's the last thing I want to happen. I've been so happy with Jeff since meeting him, but I still feel like he's hiding things from me."

"That's because he is," Marlon said.

"Marlon!" Laurel said. "Don't say shit like that!"

"I wouldn't say it if it wasn't true," he said.

"And I believe you," I replied. I shook my head as I stood in front of them. "What should I do? Confront him? Because he did it again."

"Again?" Laurel said. She looked at Marlon.

"Yeah, it's time to confront him . . . if you wanna lose him," he replied.

"What?!" I said.

"You heard me," he said as he held a slight grin.

Laurel looked at him and slightly lowered her head.

"Well, why?" I asked.

"Because what he does is none of your business, that's why," he informed me.

"Well, I think it is her business," Laurel said.

"Yeah, me too. I agree with Laurel. I'm his girlfriend now, I should be able to talk to him about anything."

"And that's exactly why you shouldn't. You're just his girlfriend, Liz, not his wife, and if you wanna make it to wife status then I encourage you to listen to me. If you become a whiny, nagging girlfriend, what makes him think that you'll be any better as a wife? You'll end up worse, especially living the life that you're living with him. You see how much he spoils you already. Any woman can get used to being spoiled very quick," he said, and glared at Laurel.

"What the hell are you looking at me for? I don't whine or nag and I'm *not* spoiled!"

"No, not that much anymore, but I beg to differ about being spoiled because don't think I forgot about the car incident in the driveway where you thought Liz's new car was yours."

"Fuck you, Marlon," she said with a smirk.

"Anytime, baby!" he replied with a sexy grin.

We all laughed.

"Well, anyway, I don't wanna be what you're saying, Marlon, and I don't think I am since I've gotten this far with him despite his jealous ex-girlfriend and her friends and just shit I see on social media about our relationship that I haven't even told you both about. This is the happiest I've been in years and I wanna stay this way."

"Then remember what I said," he warned me.

Several minutes later I was upstairs in my bedroom with my door closed and flipping through channels on my new 4K TV, courtesy of Jeff. I knew I was the luckiest woman in this world to be his girlfriend and felt very spoiled at that, but I wasn't sure if I was gonna make it to wife status; that was reality. Jeff could have any woman he wanted and could meet a new girl tomorrow that he instantly fell for, and where would that leave me? I had to do whatever I could to keep him, but the texts and all the other mess just wouldn't get the hell out of my mind, and I knew there was a reason why. I'd thought about what Jeff said in terms of how it could very well not be a woman who was doing this, and I now knew exactly who I needed to talk to.

CHAPTER NINETEEN

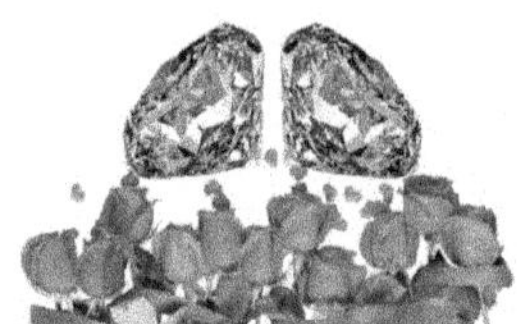

"Wow, you actually showed. I thought you were kidding at first about wanting to come over here. This must be pretty damn serious. C'mon in," Devin said.

I walked into his house with full caution. "So, is your girlfriend really out of town? I don't wanna get surprised while I'm here."

"She's out of town, Liz. I wouldn't lie to you about that. We have the whole house to ourselves. Sorry it doesn't measure up to a 20,000 square-foot mansion that your new boyfriend lives in."

I shook my head. "Well, I didn't come here to compare Jeff's house to yours, Devin, you know that."

He grinned. "Yeah, I know."

We sat down in the family room.

"Want anything to drink?"

"Yeah, just a Canada Dry," I replied as I stared at the TV.

"Still your favorite, huh?"

"Yeah," I replied with a slight smile.

"Be right back."

He gave me my drink minutes later and I didn't wanna waste a second more about talking to him about what I wanted to talk about. "So, what brings you here?"

I sighed. "Look, before I go into this, I want you to know that I'm not accusing you of anything, okay? I'm just asking."

He grinned and then took a sip of his hard liquor. "You haven't asked me anything yet."

"Yeah, I know, I was just getting to it."

And this was the kind of smart-ass sarcasm I couldn't stand about him and one of the many reasons why we weren't together anymore.

"Well, as you know, me being with Jeff hasn't been all what people think it is."

"I thought you were happy?"

I sighed once again as I stared at the TV. "Well, yeah, I'm very happy, but I'm never gonna be fully happy if I just don't find out something."

"And what is that?" he asked, and took another swig of his drink.

I pulled my phone out of my purse and showed him the texts.

"Damn," he said, as he scrolled through them. He gave my phone back to me. "Sounds like a hater, Liz. But what do you reasonably expect when you're the girlfriend of a billionaire and a black one at that?"

"Yeah, I know that, but I know the difference between someone who's just trolling or whatever, and a person who is seriously hellbent on ruining my relationship with Jeff. Jeff has made me very happy since our breakup and I wanna stay this way."

"Then ignore that shit," he suggested. "That's what I would do." He sighed. "Liz, I don't think you realize just how lucky you are to even be the girlfriend of someone like Jeff. I'm not saying that you don't deserve him, it's just that you're too damn worried about shit that you shouldn't be worried about. If I was with a billionaire or even one myself, the last thing I'll be worried about is some fuckin' hatin'-ass troll who has nothing better to do with their time and will never measure up to you or Jeff in any way, shape, or form. People are just fucked up out here, Liz. You're one of the last people who has to worry about some stupid texts from a person who's just trying to end things between you and Jeff. Enjoy yourself with a man like him. Stay happy, damn."

I nodded with a slight smile. "Yeah, I know, Devin. But you know I have to ask—"

"If I'm the one doing this shit to you, Liz? Is that it? Are you fuckin' serious?"

I started to feel bad that I'd even considered him. "Well, you are my ex, and you know what they say."

"Well, *I* say that I didn't send those to you. Why the fuck would I do some shit like that?"

"Because you're my ex. The ex is always usually the first suspect. I thought it was Jeff's ex Karis that was sending them, until another text came in while me, Jeff, and Jenelle were standing there confronting her about it."

"That Jenelle is finer than a motherfuck!"

"She's gay as a motherfuck," I informed him with a grin.

"No she's not," he replied.

"Yeah, she is, and she doesn't hide it. You have no chance with her if you tried to talk to her. There's not a man in this world she wants, and like how her brother can have any woman he wants, well, so can she."

He grinned. "Well, it would've been worth a try if I wasn't in love with Pilar and our baby that's on the way."

"I don't wanna hear this, okay?"

"You came over here, Liz."

"Yeah, and it was to talk to you about these texts, not to talk about your love for your pregnant girlfriend and baby."

"Jealous?" he said with a grin.

"Fuck you," I angrily replied. "I have nothing to be jealous of. I'm Jeff Vick's girlfriend, one of only two black billionaires in this whole world in his age range. No one has got the kind of man I got."

"Then why are you really over here?"

"I told you why!" I angrily replied. I started to feel a really bad headache come on, and it was rare that I got them. "Look, I better get going. I'm not gonna sit here and argue with you all night. Either you're lying to me about being the one who's sending me these texts or you're not, and it's on your conscience if you are. I did my part in asking you. But if you say you love your pregnant girlfriend so much then fine, maybe it isn't you. But let me tell you something—you, nor anyone else out there, is gonna ruin my relationship with Jeff, and I mean that!"

I quickly got up . . . and quickly sat back down.

He gave me a look of concern. "Are you all right, Liz?"

I put my hand on my forehead. "I'm starting to feel dizzy and nauseous. I think I may have to sit here for a while to let it pass."

"You can stay here as long as you want. Remember, Pilar is out of town and is not expected back here until tomorrow, and I'm not expecting anyone tonight, so just relax."

I stared at him as he looked like a blur to me. His voice started to become a bunch of mumbling word salad to me as well. I just didn't know why I'd started to feel this way all of the sudden, but I felt myself starting to lose consciousness, and that's the last thing I wanted to do, especially over an ex-boyfriend's house.

I felt him pull me up off of the couch. "Where are you taking me?"

"To my bedroom. You need to lay down and you'll be more comfortable there like you were when we were together."

Everything looked even more like a blur to me as he led me to his bedroom. I laid down on his bed and completely lost consciousness.

I woke up the next day . . . still in Devin's bed. "SHIT!" I said and jumped up. I looked around for my shoes and put them on and grabbed my purse. I rushed out the door to Devin walking down the hall with a tray of food.

"Good morning. I made you some breakfast."

"Sorry, I need to get out of here. You'll have to eat it yourself."

"I already ate," he informed me.

"Well, too bad. I can't." I looked at my phone and saw several calls from Laurel, but none from Jeff. "Thanks for the talk last night and letting me sleep off my bad headache. Bye."

He nodded with a smile. "Bye."

Several minutes later, I walked through the door of my home while Laurel was about to leave for work. "Hey."

"Hey. Were you at Jeff's all last night?"

I hung my head in shame. "No, I wasn't. I was at Devin's."

"DEVIN'S?!"

"Shhhh!" I said, as I looked around to see if anyone was outside. "Look, I had to know if he was the one sending me the texts, and he said he wasn't."

"Do you believe him?"

I shrugged. "I honestly don't know. I kind of do, but then again he could've been lying. I only stayed over there because I came down with a really bad headache while I was there so I just slept it off there. His girlfriend is out of town and supposed to be coming back later on today."

She nodded. "Well, I need to get to work, Liz. Some of us have real problems and bills to pay and don't have the option of quitting our jobs because a billionaire made us their significant other."

I sighed. "Well, you know it hasn't been all pure bliss, Laurel. I still have problems and so does Jeff. I haven't talked to him since yesterday morning, and we usually would talk once before then. I know he has a lot of shareholders meetings and everything so I try not to bother him because he takes these meetings seriously since he does his research before going to them because it's how he made his billions. But I'm just gonna go in here and take a shower and get something to eat and probably go back to sleep. Have a nice day at work."

"Yeah . . . right," she said with a smirk.

CHAPTER TWENTY

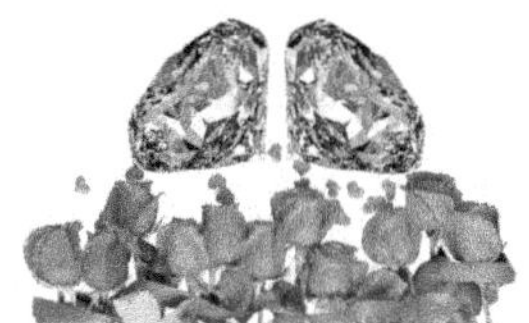

"Liz."

I jumped up out of a deep sleep to find Jeff staring down at me.

"Jeff! Oh, my God! How did you get in here?"

"Laurel let me in. I called her since I tried to call you and I wasn't getting an answer. She saw on the app on her phone that your car was still in the driveway so she let me in."

I wrestled myself up and sat at the side of the bed. I grabbed my phone off of my nightstand. "Sorry, I see you did try to call. What's the matter?"

He stared down at me. I knew something was wrong. He took out his phone as he shook his head. "When did this happen?" he asked, and showed me what he was talking about.

It was a picture of me and Devin in bed together!

"WHAT?!" I said, as I jumped out of bed. "Where the fuck did you get that from?!"

"Doesn't matter where I got it from, Liz. How long have you been seeing your ex again behind my back?"

"Jeff, I'm *not* seeing him again, okay?"

"Well, this picture says otherwise, Liz. You can't deny that it's you in this picture and you can't deny that it's your ex, now can you?"

I lowered my head. "No, I can't."

He sighed. "When did this happen?"

"Nothing happened, Jeff! Nothing! *I swear* nothing did!"

And I was telling the truth. I knew Devin and I didn't do a damn thing last night and I had a hundred percent clear conscience about it, but it was clear he had other things in mind once I got there.

"I'm finding this very hard to believe, Liz. I couldn't get a hold of you all last night and then someone anonymously texts this to me this afternoon showing a picture of you laying up in bed with your ex? You only have one more chance to admit to the obvious or else we're gonna have a problem."

Tears welled up in my eyes. "I'm not admitting to anything I didn't do, Jeff. All I will admit to is that I was over his house last night, but I didn't have sex with him, okay?"

He started to pace in my room as he shook his head while he still held his phone by his side. "What the hell were you doing over there?"

I sighed. "I needed to ask him about these texts that I've been receiving from someone who doesn't want to see me happy; see us happy. I have to eliminate everyone, Jeff. I did think he was the one doing this after we eliminated Karis but he told me he isn't and I don't know if I a hundred percent believe him or not. I just want this shit to stop and the only way I'm gonna get it to stop is if I start asking around about who's doing this. This shit isn't happening to you, it's happening to me!"

"How did the two of end up in bed together, Liz? I'm sure it wasn't for him to console you about these texts you were asking him about."

"No it wasn't, Jeff. I had a real bad migraine come on really fast while I was over there because I was so stressed about these texts and everything and have been since I've been getting them. He just took me to his bedroom and told me to lay down in his bed until I felt better enough to go home and that's what I did. He obviously took this picture of him in the bed with me when I was sleeping because I didn't wake up until early today. I didn't know he did that until you showed me just now."

He stared at me as if he didn't know whether or not he should've believed me. "I don't know what to think about this, Liz. And things were going so good between us."

"What do you mean?"

"I mean that I just can't accept the fact that you were over your ex's house just to talk about these texts you've been receiving. You could've talked to him about this over the phone—am I right?"

I lowered my head. "Yeah, you're right."

"So why didn't you?"

"Because I wanted to see his reaction to what I had to ask him and I wanted to see it in person since I rarely do FaceTime. I don't know why you're making a big deal out of this, Jeff."

"So you don't think this is a big deal? I get a text of a picture of you in bed with your ex and you admitted to me that you were over his house last night."

"And where were you last night because I couldn't get a hold of you just like you couldn't get a hold of me!"

"After the shareholders meeting I was at home all night, Liz, trying to get a hold of you."

"Well, like you told me, I couldn't get a hold of you last night just as much as you couldn't get a hold of me."

"Why are we talking in circles? I don't have to explain to you where I'm at or what I'm doing all of the time. When I tell you something then I expect for you to believe me. I'm being truthful with you so I expect for you to be truthful with me."

"*I am,* Jeff! I just don't want you thinking that I'm fucking my ex when I'm not. I went over there to talk to him, I got a migraine from the stress of it all, I laid in his bed to let it pass and I didn't wake up until the next day. That was some dirty shit he did by taking a pic of us in bed as if we did sleep together. I don't know what else to say about it because there is nothing else to say about it because I know for a fact that nothing happened."

He sighed as he shook his head. "I need some time, Liz."

I looked at him. "Some time for what, Jeff?"

"I need some time for myself already, and I didn't think I was gonna have to say this and say this so soon."

“Say what, Jeff?”

“We need to take a break from each other,” he informed me.

I felt weak all over. I fell back on my bed. “What are you *really saying,* Jeff?”

“I said what I said, Liz. I don’t wanna talk about this anymore. I’ll let myself out.” He turned around and quickly walked out of my room.

I managed to get up even though I felt weak in the knees. I breathed heavy as tears welled up in my eyes as I watched him walk out the door, get into his car, and leave. “JEFF!!!!!!” I screamed, and collapsed to the floor.

CHAPTER TWENTY-ONE

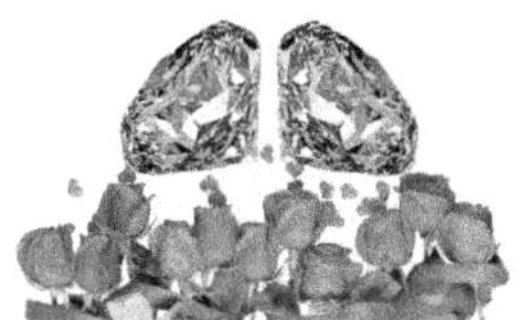

"I don't even know if I'm still his girlfriend," I said as I wept through half of a box of newly opened tissues.

Laurel handed me a cup of hot tea. "Did he say the two of you weren't together anymore?" she asked, as she sat down in a chair in front of my bed as Marlon sat at a chair at my desk.

"No, he didn't say it. He just said he needed some time to himself and that we needed a break from each other. All because of a fuckin' picture that Devin took of me and him while I was sleeping off my migraine in his bed. I know nothing happening between the two of us! I know it! I have a clear conscience about it!" I said, and blew my nose as I sat on my bed.

"We believe you, Liz. Right, Marlon?"

He grinned as he looked at his phone.

"*Right,* Marlon?!" Laurel said again.

I looked at him as tears streamed from my eyes.

"Sure, we believe you, Liz. Never liked Devin; always thought there was something about him. He was very sneaky and that was some sneaky-ass shit he did. I'm sorry, Liz."

I shook my head. "He's gonna get it for this. He quite possibly ruined my relationship with the best man I've ever, *ever* been with. He did this shit because he didn't wanna see me happy, that's the only reason why he did it; telling me that I shouldn't be worried about those texts and about other things since I was with Jeff—but look what the fuck he did? Did he think this shit was funny or something? And then he sent it to Jeff obviously pretending to be someone else!"

"Now I don't know about that, Liz," Marlon said.

I looked at him. "What do you mean?"

"I don't think he sent it to Jeff. Someone else probably did," he informed me.

"Well, whoever did just doesn't wanna see me happy. I never knew how many fuckin' haters there were out here until I started dating Jeff, and now my ex-boyfriend wanted to get in on this shit by taking a picture like *this*?! I'm sorry, Marlon, but I can't believe he *didn't* send this to him."

"Did Jeff tell you it was Devin who sent it to him?" he asked.

"No, he told me it was sent to him anonymously. Now the fuckin' picture is everywhere! I look like a cheating girlfriend when I'm anything but that! Hell, I never cheated on Devin when I was with him but now he wanted to make it look as if I cheated on Jeff with him? Now I may have lost Jeff over this! I just don't know why he won't believe me when I told him nothing happened between Devin and me! I've been completely faithful to him. Why the fuck would I fuck up and fuck my ex when I have someone like Jeff Vick?"

"That's a good question," Laurel said.

I looked at Marlon as he looked at his phone. "Marlon?"

"What?" he asked, as he looked up at me.

"What do you think about all of this?"

He sighed. "Just hope for the best, Liz."

"So, it's over between Jeff and Liz. Told you it wasn't gonna last," Beverly said, as she and Karis and Chloe sat outside in her backyard by the pool.

"Couldn't resist cheating with that broke-ass ex of hers," Chloe said, and took a sip of her drink.

"He's actually pretty nice looking, but doesn't measure up to my high standards," Beverly said. "But, Karis, you're on your way to getting Jeff back once and for all. You said he called you today, right?"

"Yeah, he did. I was surprised to hear from him," Karis replied. "He just wanted to say he was sorry again for accusing me of sending those texts to Liz, and that he'll talk to me later."

"Well, if he said he was gonna talk to you later and most of all apologized *again* for accusing you of that crap then it's clear he wants to talk to you about getting back together," Chloe said with a smile.

Karis smiled in return. "I think so too."

"I think Jeff knew the kind of mistake he made in making Liz his girlfriend. Like we all know and have always known, she doesn't fit in anyone's circles. He was just trying to save a woman from her miserable, low-class life by giving her a chance of a lifetime to be with someone like him . . . and now it's over. He had his fun and now he's over her. It's clear that he wants more out of a relationship and with someone who he should've never left to begin with, and that's *you,* Karis," Beverly said.

"And I can't wait to tell the world when we are back together," Karis said.

Jeff's best friend Grant handed him a drink as they sat in Jeff's recreation room while they watched a game. "Thanks, man," he said.

"You're welcome," he replied with a smile and sat on the couch with him.

Jeff shook his head. "I honestly don't know what to think about this, man. I think in a lot of ways that Liz is telling the truth about not sleeping with her ex, but you know I just don't really know that for sure."

"How come?" Grant asked, and took a sip of drink.

"Because I don't know the true extent of her relationship with him. They were together for years and I just don't know if she still has some lingering feelings for him."

"True, man. But I don't understand why any woman would have any feelings for their ex if they have you as a man."

"I'm just a man, I feel," Jeff said, as he passively stared at the TV.

"It's clear that someone's feelings can totally take over them and they just can't get over them like the way they thought they could or thought they did since she told me she was completely over him. Maybe seeing him again at his house in person brought all of that out of her when she saw him."

"Maybe, maybe not, man. But I think she's telling you the truth that she didn't do anything with him."

He looked at him. "How come?"

"Liz seems like an honest person, unlike Karis who's just a nasty-ass bitch for the streets who was fucking so many men behind your back and thinking that she could still keep a man like you. Liz is a real one, Jeff. I don't think you would've given her that many roses at that concert that night and made her your girlfriend so fast if you thought she was for the streets like Karis and most women out there."

He nodded. "Yeah, you're right, man. It was something about Liz that stood out to me that night. She just looked so unhappy and lonely, and she told me that she was. She had no idea who I was, either, and that's always a plus. I know I haven't been honest with her about everything that's been going on with me, either."

Grant stared at him. "You mean she doesn't know?"

"No, she doesn't know, man. And I just don't know at this point if I should tell her or not because I just don't know what direction I wanna take our relationship in now. I just can't be a hundred percent sure she was not over her ex's house for other reasons than what she said she was over there for."

"True, man. But it's up to you about what you wanna do. I can't make any relationship decisions for you."

Jeff's phone rang. He looked at it. "Hey," he answered, as he stayed seated. "Yeah, I think we do need to talk. C'mon over."

CHAPTER TWENTY-TWO

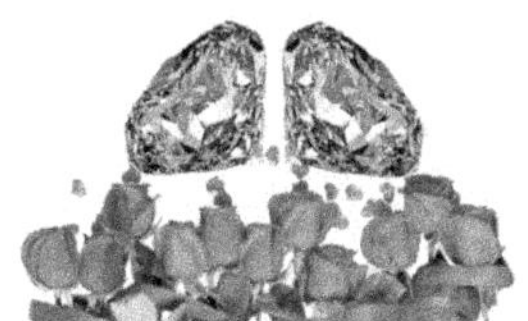

I walked through the hall and into the kitchen with Laurel behind me. I wanted her to get everything on video as well as I needed her for moral support. I reached the kitchen to a colorful array of bluish hues everywhere in the form of streamers and confetti, as well as a huge cake.

Gender reveal party.

It's a boy . . .

For Devin and his girlfriend Pilar.

But I wasn't here to celebrate anything with anyone. I was here for answers and I was not leaving until I got them and I was satisfied with what he had to tell me about why he did what he did. It was clear he could celebrate his unborn child, but was clearly hellbent on ruining my life and a possible marriage and family I could have in the future with Jeff, and I wanted to know why.

"Liz! Hey, girl. What are you doing here?" Devin asked, as everyone else looked stunned to see me here, especially his friends and family.

It was as if I didn't know any of them anymore, but I wasn't here to make amends with anyone because I never did anything wrong and never disrespected any of them, and they knew it. I was in a whole other relationship with someone else—or at least I'd hoped that I still was—so I wanted to know why he was trying to ruin it.

"You know damn well why I'm here, Devin," I replied as I tried my hardest not to get loud.

He grinned as he looked around at everyone as if he was embarrassed that I'd showed up here and especially at a party like this. "No, Liz, I actually don't know why you're here."

"Don't you play dumb with me!" I said, as I tried to contain my composure because as usual, he was really trying my patience and knew exactly how to do it.

"What's going on?" Pilar asked as she walked up to him and slowly held on to his hand.

"Liz came here to congratulate us," Devin said with a smile.

"Cut the shit, Devin!" I said.

Everyone gasped as some laughed, but I was in no mood for any of this.

I shoved my phone in his face. "Why the hell did you take this picture of us and send it to Jeff?"

Pilar tried to look at it but before she could, he shoved it back to me. "I didn't send that to him, Liz. And I took that for fun."

"Oh, yeah?! *So funny,* Devin, ha ha! Someone sent him that picture and it was clear that it was you so don't start this lying with me! I'm not in the mood for it! You could've quite possibly ruined my relationship with Jeff and it's like you don't even care! How could you do this to me?! Do you really think I care about your relationship and all that's going on with you right now? Why did you do this to me?"

He sighed as he shook his head. "Liz. I'm only gonna say this one more time. Yes, I took the picture, but no, I did not send it to Jeff. Now you can believe what you wanna believe, okay? But right now there's a party going on and you and Laurel are welcomed to stay if you want."

"Let's go," I said to Laurel.

Minutes later, Laurel drove my car back home since I was too upset to drive there and back home. "So, do you believe him?"

I shook my head as tears streamed from my eyes. "I just can't get myself to believe him, Laurel. I think he was saying that shit because he was in front of all of his friends and family as well as hers and didn't wanna look like some cheater. I know we didn't do anything with each other, but that picture suggests that we did and I know that's exactly what he wanted people to think. Someone sent that picture to Jeff, and Devin is the most obvious person!"

"Well, you know how someone can take a picture and send it to someone and it could be everywhere within seconds. Maybe Devin sent it to a friend or something and he sent it to someone else and it obviously ended up getting sent to Jeff. There's a lot of scenarios, Liz, too many to count."

"Yeah, I know there is, Laurel, and I'm just mad that he would even joke about something like this because he's always been a fuckin' jokester, but this is not funny at all because there are some things you just don't joke about and this is one of them. He fucked with my relationship with Jeff doing this shit. It's just taking a picture like that alone would make people think I was cheating on Jeff with him, and I know that's exactly how he wanted it to look."

"Yeah, I know he did. And his ass was so fake in there as well. He really took a nosedive in women ever since the two of you broke up. That chick he's with right now looks like she belongs to the streets."

"Well, I don't know her or wanna know her. All I know is that she better now realize who she has because everything is not all fun and games. Like I said, he fucked with my relationship with Jeff doing that shit. Motherfucker just didn't think a relationship between Jeff and me was gonna last this long and be this serious so fast, but this is what happens when two people connect so well, and I don't know if that connection has been permanently broken now!" I cried even harder.

Laurel consoled me while we were at a stoplight. "It's okay, Liz. You just need to do whatever you can to keep Jeff. He didn't tell you that it was over between the two of you, right?"

"Right," I sobbed.

"Then it's not over. Like you told me what he said, he just needs some time, that's all. We'll get to the bottom of who sent that picture to Jeff because for some reason, Liz, now when I think about it, I'm just not a hundred percent sure it was Devin like what I originally thought as well."

"How come?"

"I don't know; can't really put my finger on it. He was really calm about it when you confronted him. Yeah, I know it could've been different if he was there by himself but he actually conducted himself in a calm manner and it was just something about it all that had me convinced that even though he took the picture, he didn't send it to Jeff."

"But he obviously sent to someone, Laurel! And he did that because he doesn't wanna see me happy. He tried to act as if he was so supportive of me and Jeff's relationship, but who the fuck takes a selfie of themselves in bed with their ex when we're both now in different relationships? Now that was starting shit and he knows it!"

She grinned. "Yeah, you're right, Liz. That's definitely starting shit. But you see how he didn't want his girl to see the pic."

"I'm sure she's seen it; she just hasn't said anything to him about it."

"Yeah, I think she has as well. But have you tried to talk to Jeff since?"

"Yeah, I called him once before we went to Devin's because I wanted to let him know I was going there to confront him about the picture—but he didn't answer. He knew it was me. I tried to text him as well and I know he saw those as well; he was just ignoring them. I don't wanna keep calling and texting and emailing him or whatever because then I would start to look crazy and I don't wanna look like that at all. But I just don't wanna go too long without talking to him. I already miss him, Laurel. I just never thought I would feel this way about another man so fast, and it's not because he's a billionaire. Jeff and I have real feelings for each other, but now I really don't know how he feels about me anymore!"

Once again, I broke down and cried and she tried her best to console me.

Jeff and Grant watched the video titled: Billionaire Jeff Vick's Girlfriend Liz Green Confronts Ex-Boyfriend Devin About Viral Sexy Photo of the Two of Them in Bed.

Grant divided his attention between the video and to Jeff's reaction to it. The video ended. "So, what do you think, man?"

"I didn't think she would do anything like this," Jeff honestly replied. "It's clear she's very upset about this picture getting out, but how do I know if she's doing this just so it doesn't look like she did anything with him? I can't prove that she did do anything with him and I can't tell her who to see, but why talk to your ex about those texts, you know? She was with him for five years; we haven't even been with each other for five months. I just don't know if she's really being truthful about not having any feelings for him anymore. Five years is a long time to be with someone. Some people aren't even married for that long anymore."

"Yeah, you're right about that, man," Grant replied. "So, since we saw her confront her ex about this, I feel she's telling the truth about not sleeping with him. Maybe he's the type that likes to start shit and he started some shit all right with doing what he did."

A drink was handed to Jeff. "Thank you."

"You're welcome."

"So, it seems like you can't trust Liz as much as you thought you could and I know trust is everything to you," Grant said.

"Yeah, it pretty much is," Jeff said, and took a sip of his drink.

"So, what's going on, man?" Grant asked.

Jeff sighed. "I have a lot to think about; got a lot on my mind. Liz is still my girlfriend, I just told her I need some time for myself; she thought I was breaking up with her. I just need to find out more about this. I see she confronted him but that doesn't prove that she didn't sleep with him. I just don't know what to think, man. I just think she's taking these texts and in her quest to find out who's sending them to her a little too far."

"But don't you wanna know who's sending them to her? It's clear it's someone who doesn't want the two of you together. Do you believe it's her ex?"

Jeff sighed once again. "I have to be honest. I don't think it's him. There's no telling who it is. I told her to ignore them, block them and everything, but she wanted to play detective because she told me that whosever sending them is fucking with our relationship and she doesn't feel that she can really move forward in it if she doesn't find this out."

"Well, I feel there's always gonna be haters when it comes to any relationship you're in, Jeff, it's just that Liz happens to be getting the brunt of it because people just don't think the two of you belong together."

"Well, I don't know why people think that, but now I just don't know what to think about our relationship anymore."

CHAPTER TWENTY-THREE

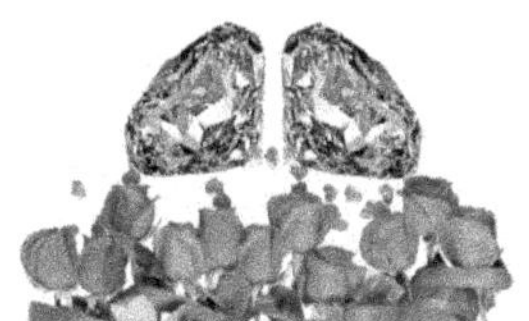

Weeks had gone by—might as well have been months—since Jeff and I had talked. It was clear he needed this time away from me and he was serious about it. I just didn't know where the two of stood anymore. I felt I didn't have a boyfriend anymore. I also felt he didn't believe my side of the story when it came to the infamous picture, and this was showing me he had trust issues with me.

I thought about all of this as I sat in Autumn's room as we had our monthly Auntie and Niece Night, and for the millionth time it seemed, we watched *The Princess and the Frog,* one of her favorite movies, since she couldn't decide on anything new she wanted to see.

She looked up at me. "Aunt Lizzie, why do you look so sad?"

Wow. She noticed. I couldn't even hide it even though I was trying my hardest to.

"I'm just tired, baby. That's all," I lied.

"Do you wanna go to sleep? It's okay. I'll stay up and watch."

I smiled. "It's okay, baby. I'm not gonna go to sleep on you."

"Aunt Lizzie."

"Yes, baby?"

"Princesses are supposed to be happy, that's why I chose this movie to watch again and wanted to know why you look so sad."

I looked at her in total shock. "What? Well, honey, they can get sad, too. They have feelings. But why are you referring to me as a princess?"

"Because you're with Jeff and he's a prince because he lives in a palace so you're a princess. I wish I was you, Aunt Lizzie."

Wow.

Just wow.

My only niece was mistaking me as being a princess because I was with Jeff and she equated that to happiness.

"Well, honey, no matter what walk of life a woman is from, she can always be a princess; she doesn't have to be with someone as wealthy as Jeff. And no one is happy a hundred percent of the time although most of us would like to be, but we can increase our chances of being happy by being around those who make us happy and who are uplifting and inspiring to us."

"That's what Mommy and Daddy say."

"Well, they're right, honey. You have great parents."

I wanted to tell her that life was no fairytale, but I felt that was her parents responsibility to explain all of that to her, not me. But she was seeing firsthand that someone close to her was living the life of a princess therefore she identified me as one. I had to admit that it'd been as close to a fairytale as I was gonna ever get with the moment I'd met Jeff and the times we've had together, but I just didn't know now if all of that had come to an end; he was just trying to find a way to tell me.

CHAPTER TWENTY-FOUR

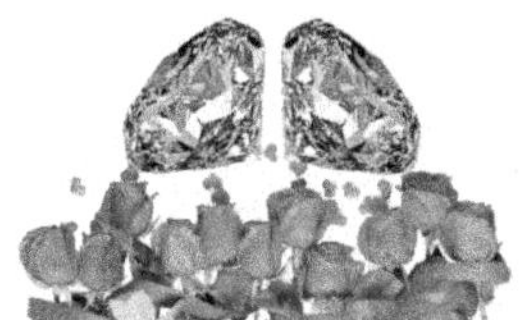

"Jenelle, where are you?" Jeff asked, as he walked up the beautiful spiral staircase of Jenelle's home. He headed down the hall towards her bedroom. "Jenelle? Where are you?" he asked again as he approached her door. He knocked on it once and opened it to her having a lot of butt-naked fun with a woman who was not her girlfriend. "Oh, God!"

The woman jumped under the covers as Jenelle grinned.

"What's up, big bro? How come you didn't tell me you were coming over?" she asked, as she grabbed her robe that was on the floor by her bed.

"I just wanted to come over and talk, but I see you're busy."

"Not anymore. Meet me in the kitchen. I'll make us some coffee."

Minutes later, they sat at the kitchen table with their mugs of hot coffee. Jenelle told the woman she was fooling around with to go home.

"So, I take that this is about Liz?" she asked, and sipped her coffee.

"Yeah, it is," he replied, as he stared down into his mug.

"Well, I have to admit I was shocked when I saw that picture of her with her ex. I didn't think she would cheat on you with him . . . and I still don't think she did."

He looked up at her. "Well, that's not the way the picture looked to me. I just don't understand why she would do this if she really did. She's the first woman that I have really felt something special with, now I don't know how I feel anymore."

She nodded. "Jeff. I've seen as well how happy you've been with her and I can tell she's been the same with you. If she really did do this then it was a serious lapse in judgement on her part. It's clear that she still had some feelings for her ex, and when she saw him in person all of those feelings just came out. It happens. You've cheated on all of your ex-girlfriends and so have I."

"Yeah, I know, Jenelle, but I've never cheated on Liz, that's when I knew I had someone special. I know she appreciates everything I've given her, but since doing this to me I just feel that she totally disrespected me and our relationship because she did. I also feel that she's being too damn paranoid about some texts that she keeps receiving when she knows damn well as I do that it's nothing but a damn hater sending them to her. A lot of people don't wanna see us together and I kept trying to explain to her that it comes with the territory of being with someone like me but I just don't seem to be getting through to her, and I really believe that now."

"Someone like you," she said with a grin, and took another sip of her coffee. "Conceited much?"

"Jenelle," he said with a slight grin himself. "You know how it is with me. The last thing I am is conceited. My status as a black man is unlike most black men, and no one can deny that."

"Yeah, you're right."

"So, with my status comes along with the fact that I have to choose my friends and the women I get involved with very carefully."

"And is there something you're not telling me or Liz, Jeff? Because I just think those texts that she's receiving have some kind of connection to you."

He shook his head. "I don't know what kind of connection they have to me if they even have any connection at all. I'm just as confused about who could be sending them just as much as you, Liz, and everyone else is. I just don't want her losing her mind over this but it seems as if she already has, and I'm not gonna deal with a crazy woman."

"Liz is not crazy, Jeff, and you know that as well otherwise you would've never made her your girlfriend. I really, truly like her, and you know you don't hear that coming from me that often at all when it comes to the women you get involved with. I never liked any of your girlfriends from the past, but I like Liz. She's a good woman. She's real; authentic. If it's true that she did cheat on you then I'm sure there is a very good reason why she did it and you shouldn't end your relationship with her over it. But like I said, I don't think she did; she just doesn't seem like the type that cheats on her man, especially a man like you."

"Well, I hope you're right about everything you're saying, Jenelle. Liz is the best girlfriend I've had, and we've had some pretty incredible months together, but there are some decisions that I have to make."

"And I know you'll make the right ones."

CHAPTER TWENTY-FIVE

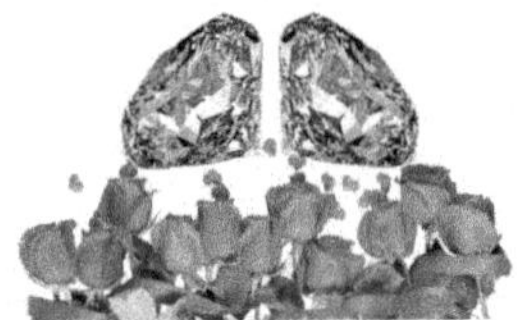

"LIZ!"

I jumped out of my bed to Laurel shaking me as Marlon stood by her side. "What?! What is it?"

"You know I don't mean to wake you up unless it's something that I have to wake you up for," she replied in a serious tone as her voice cracked.

"What? What are you talking about?" I asked.

Something about the way she looked had me very concerned. I'd never seen her look like this before. She looked as if she wanted to tell me something but was too afraid to do it. I looked at Marlon.

"What the hell is going on?" I asked the two of them. "Marlon?"

"She needs to tell you, Liz," he replied.

Laurel took a deep breath. She showed me her phone:

<u>BREAKING NEWS!</u>

Billionaire Jeff Vick Engaged to Thirst-Trap Social Media Model Chrissie Lissette

I dropped Laurel's phone on the floor. I didn't even wanna click it on.

"Liz. We know you'll never get over this, and we're here for you," Laurel said, as she tried to give me one of the most sympathetic looks that she'd ever given me.

"Absolutely," Marlon agreed.

I grabbed my keys and stormed out of my room.

"LIZ! WHERE ARE YOU GOING?!" Laurel yelled as she and Marlon ran after me.

I got into my car and left.

I honestly didn't know where I was going. My first thought was to go talk to Jeff about this, but I just couldn't get myself to do it. This was the ultimate betrayal. I felt like I was in a nightmare, but this was a wide-awake reality for me. I couldn't believe this was happening. The best relationship I'd ever been in. Ever.

And it was all a lie.

He didn't care about me at all. I was just another woman he just wanted to have his fun with. He tricked me. He tricked me good and I couldn't see any of this for what it was worth. It was clear he was more concerned with wanting to be with some fake-ass fuckin' model than being with someone who really liked him and cared for him.

At this point I wish I'd never met him.

He couldn't even be a man about it and tell me he was even seeing someone else the same time he was seeing me, obviously, but I was the one who ultimately lost out on a chance to be with him forever.

I pulled into a well-lit mini mall with fast-food restaurants and parked my car in the corner. I got out my phone and got ready to call Jeff. I shook my head and slammed my phone down on the passenger's seat. I just didn't wanna talk to him right now; I didn't wanna talk to anyone right now. He really made me look like a fool; made our whole relationship look like what I now know what it was—fake. Made up. I was just a temporary stop on his quest to get who he really wanted, and who he really wanted showed me his true colors after all.

I couldn't believe I was used like this.

And to think I went through all of that shit cussing Devin out for acting as if we'd slept together and sending it to Jeff. I still thought he had something to do with it, but it was clear it didn't matter who had what to do with anything now.

Jeff and I were through, and he didn't even have the heart to tell me.

Two-hundred roses . . . was all a lie.

Fancy car . . . was all a lie.

Expensive clothes, shoes, bags, jewelry . . . was all a lie.

Exotic trips all over the world . . . was all a lie.

Everything was a lie.

I couldn't think about any of this anymore. This was the worst that it'd gotten, and now I was gonna have to hear about how another woman was gonna be living a life that I'd dreamed to live like millions and millions of other women; that I did live like while being his temporary girlfriend as I was now calling it, and this was only the beginning.

Over an hour later, I decided to go home.

I walked through the garage door as Laurel ran up to me.

"Liz. There's someone here to see you."

"I don't wanna see anyone right now."

"Liz—"

"Laurel! Please! *I said* I don't wanna see anyone right now! You know how upset I am. Whoever it is, tell them to get the fuck out of —" I looked up.

Jeff was standing in the kitchen as Marlon stood next to him. "Hi, Liz."

CHAPTER TWENTY-SIX

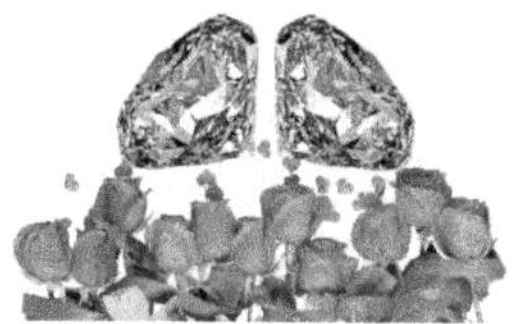

Jeff closed my bedroom door behind him as I stood on the defense in the middle of my room.

Here we were, face-to-face. We hadn't seen each other in well over a month and it felt a lot longer than that. Here was his chance to explain to me what the hell was going on with all of this.

"Sit down," he told me.

"No, I'm not sitting down, Jeff. I'm way too mad," I said, as I stood firm where I was with my arms crossed while trying to stop the tears from welling up in my eyes.

"I didn't come over here to get in a big argument about this, Liz. I wanna talk calmly about it."

"There's nothing that's gonna be calm about this conversation, Jeff, and you know it."

"Yes, there is."

Tears flowed from my eyes. "How the hell can you say that we're gonna have a calm conversation after what you did, Jeff? Huh?"

"Because I didn't do what I did," he informed me.

I gasped as I wiped tears from my eyes. "What?! What the hell are you talking about, Jeff?"

He walked towards me. He lifted my chin up. "Liz. I'm only gonna say this once. I *never* asked Chrissie Lissette to be my wife. *Never*. This was obviously all made up by her. I can't help what people put out there about me, even if it is a lie."

I shook my head as I now sat on my bed. He sat right next to me. "Then why would she say some shit like that, Jeff? Why? It's obvious you were seeing her?"

"Chrissie and I never dated, Liz. You can confirm this with Jenelle, my friends, and family. I had a one-night stand with her. She told me she wanted us to start dating and I told her it just wasn't a good idea. I wanted to leave that night where we left it . . . and we did. Well, at least I did."

"Why?"

"Because of her rep of being with very wealthy men, plus, she has four kids by four different men, but she lied to me and said she only had one. You know what I told you about women with kids when I first met you."

"Yeah, I remember."

"So I didn't even want her as a girlfriend. She means nothing to me and she still doesn't. Apparently, she couldn't let that one night go that we had together and has been stalking me ever since."

I took a deep breath. It was either now or never. "Jeff."

"What, baby?"

I took another deep breath. "I noticed since I met you that you've been going off every time you got a call from someone. Did that happen to be her?"

"Yes," he confessed. "I wanted to block her when I noticed how many calls, texts, and emails she was sending to me, but my lawyers advised me against it because they said they could build a case against her for stalking because the amount she was sending was getting to a criminal point, and now they have. So each time she would call I would talk to her for no more than a few minutes to get the call recorded and hang up. I didn't want you to know what was going on because I didn't want you to have anything to do with it. When she saw me meet you that night of the show after giving you all of those roses, that's when it really started."

"So, she was there."

"Yeah, she was. And when she saw what I'd given you, she was furious. She called me constantly that night but I just ignored her calls, texts, and DMs—but I didn't delete them. See."

He showed me he had a true stalker on his hands. I shook my head as he scrolled through the text messages and all of the times she'd called him in just that one night. The night that we met. The night that changed my life. Little did I know someone was trying to ruin it from the start.

"Damn," I said as I shook my head. "I'm so sorry, Jeff. This woman is crazy. I hate for you to have someone like this obsessed with you. This is scary. And now she made this claim that the two of you are engaged? What are you gonna do about it?"

"Nothing. There's nothing I can do. My lawyers contacted that gossip rag that reported it and I can happily inform you that it's been taken down." He showed me his phone as he clicked on the link to the story, and the page came up saying that the story could not be found.

I smiled. "Wow, your lawyers are really on it, Jeff."

"That's what I pay them for," he replied with a smile. He got up off my bed and pulled me up off of it as well. "I would never, ever, do something like that to you, Liz. Some women out there get a chance of a lifetime to be with someone like me and they think it's their golden ticket for a lifetime of entitlement. I would never seriously be with anyone like Chrissie Lissette. Not even close. I don't even know why I had that one-night stand with her. After that, I knew I had to find someone serious. Someone that I could be comfortable with and not have to worry about her constantly being on social media showing off a life that I'd given her. Someone with no children and wanted to build on to what I've already built; someone who wants to leave a true legacy for our future children. Most women in this world don't qualify to be with men of my status, Liz, but you do. Like I always say, I don't mean to sound all arrogant but it's true."

I wiped tears from my eyes as I smiled. "It's not about being arrogant, Jeff. It's about protecting what's yours and being smart about the choices you make in life because when you make the wrong ones you will pay for it for the rest of your life. You've been very smart up to this point, that's why I was so devastated when Laurel showed me that link saying you were engaged to someone else and to a woman like *that* at that. I just knew right there I never knew the real you. I thought our relationship was fake; all a lie. I even said I wish I'd never met you. But something inside of me was saying, 'What if this isn't true?' But what that link to the story said was what I believed at that moment; what everyone believed, and what I know they still believe. So, let's go out there and tell everyone the truth."

"Yeah, I wanna do that right now as well because Laurel and Marlon looked as if they were about to kill me when I showed up here tonight!"

"You didn't tell them that your engagement to that woman wasn't true?"

"Well, I told them I wanted to talk about it to you and I wanted to let you know everything first. I was glad that you walked through that door when you had because I was about to run out of it!"

We laughed as there was a knock on my door.

"Come in!" I said.

Laurel opened the door as Jeff and I held each other. She smiled. "Liz, there's someone here to see you."

"Who?" I asked, since I wasn't even expecting Jeff, so I really wasn't expecting anyone else tonight. I looked at Jeff.

"Well, let's go see," he said.

We walked downstairs with Laurel and into the family room. I stopped cold.

It was Devin and Pilar.

CHAPTER TWENTY-SEVEN

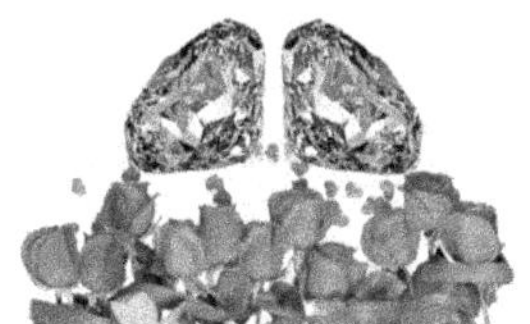

Marlon grinned as he assessed the family room as Jeff and I sat on one couch and Devin and Pilar sat on another. Laurel sat on one of the reclining chairs. "So, I didn't expect all of this. It's nice to have all the ex-boyfriends, ex-girlfriends, current boyfriends, and current girlfriends all here in one room, with a little one on the way. Could I interest anyone in something to drink or a bite to eat?"

"Knock it off, Marlon," I said, and then glared at Devin. "Devin, why are you here? There's obviously a reason."

"Yeah, there's a reason, Liz," he informed me. He looked at Pilar. "Sorry, where are my manners?"

That's an understatement, I thought.

"Everyone, this is Pilar, my girlfriend, and soon-to-be baby mama," Devin said with a grin.

"Devin," she said in a soft tone, which told me he embarrassed her by what he'd said even though it was the truth.

"Well, that's what you are," he replied with an even bigger grin, and then softly stroked her belly. "Can't wait until he's here."

Laurel crossed her arms as she tried to muster up a smile. Marlon grinned big as did Jeff.

"Um, about why you're here," I said. "It's clear it's because you wanna talk to me about something."

"Actually, Pilar wants to talk to you about something," Devin informed me.

Everyone gasped as they turned their attention to Pilar. Yeah, I couldn't wait to hear this.

"Liz, I'm really sorry for what you've been going through lately, you know, with the texts and all?" Pilar said.

I tensed up. I couldn't believe it. She was about to confess to me that she was the one who was sending me the texts!

"What about them?" I tried to say as calmly as I could.

"It's okay, baby," Jeff said, and held on to my hand and lifted it up and kissed it. Devin smirked as he shook his head.

Pilar sighed. It seemed as if this was taking a lot out of her to admit to what she'd done and I was waiting for it because I knew it was coming.

"Go on, baby, tell her what you gotta tell her," Devin said.

She sighed once again. "I know who was sending you those texts."

"Okay, who?" I asked.

"Chrissie Lissette," she confessed.

Everyone gasped, especially Jeff.

"That bitch!" Jeff said. He looked at Pilar. "And how did she get Liz's number, Pilar? It's clear that you're friends with her?"

Pilar lowered her head. "Yeah, I am. I saw it in Devin's phone and gave it to her. She said you promised her that the two of you would get back together, and when she saw that you had started a relationship with Liz, she felt hurt and betrayed."

I looked at Jeff as everyone else did to see what he had to say about this.

Jeff slightly grinned as he shook his head. "First of all, I was never in a relationship with her; she was not the type I wanted to be in a relationship with, so I never betrayed her. She was just someone I had fun with, and now the fun is over and it's just clear to me that she just can't get the fuck over it. I've told her numerous times that we were never a couple, but she couldn't take what we had for what it was, just a little fun and that was it.

"I was ready to find someone that would make me happy, someone that I could have a serious relationship with, and no social media thot is someone I wanna have a serious relationship with. I told her that, but it was clear she didn't wanna listen to me and move on like I told her to do. I told her I was not her man and never would be, so it's clear she wanted to go after the woman I was in a serious relationship with which is and still is Liz." He turned to me. "Baby, I'm so sorry this crazy thot dragged you into all of this shit. You didn't deserve this. I admit that I've gotten involved with a lot of women, but I should've known there was one that just couldn't learn how to move on, and I really don't know why she can't since she has four kids to take care of."

"And that's what I told her, Jeff," Pilar informed him. "I would tell her that you seemed happy about being with Liz and she needed to accept the fact that you were with her and to leave the two of you alone. She didn't wanna listen. She was just going on a childish rant and everything about how she deserved you more than her and everything. I was tired of hearing it. But when I saw that the media had reported that she was engaged to you I knew I had to tell Liz that she was the one sending her all of those texts and that she was not engaged to you."

"Damn fuckin' right she's not!" Jeff confirmed.

Everyone laughed.

"Well, I'm glad all of this is settled," Laurel said with a smile.

"Yeah, me too. Now we don't have to hear Liz crying in her room all day and night anymore when we're here," Marlon said.

"Marlon!" I said.

Everyone once again laughed.

"And my lawyers told all of those sites that reported my fake engagement to her to take that shit down and they did, just so you know," Jeff said to me with a smile, even though he'd already told me this in private.

"Thank you, baby," I said.

We kissed.

Devin smirked. "Well, I guess I got something to say as well."

"You *guess?*" I said.

"Let him have his say," Laurel said to me with a grin.

"Yeah, what is it?" I asked him, as my eyes narrowed on him.

"Yeah, I just wanna say that I'm sorry everyone thought Liz and I had an affair. We never did," Devin confessed.

Jeff looked at me. "You were right," he said with a smile.

"I told you!" I said with a mixture of a laugh and a little anger because I felt that he didn't believe me when I tried to tell him the truth.

"But I didn't send the picture to you, Jeff," Devin said.

"I did," Pilar confessed!

Everyone gasped as they shook their heads.

"Why were you trying to ruin my relationship with Jeff, huh? And you talked about your crazy thot friend trying to do it? What makes you so different? Huh?" I said, as I felt myself getting heated up.

"Liz, calm down," Laurel said since she could sense it as well.

"Because I thought the two of you really did sleep together. I got Jeff's number from Chrissie," Pilar said.

I shook my head. "Well, as you see Devin confessed that we never did have an affair so you did that shit for nothing."

"I know, Liz, and I'm sorry," Pilar said.

"Sorry my ass," I replied.

"What?!" Pilar said in an offensive tone.

"Okay, okay. She said she was sorry. Everything has been confessed and is out in the open so I think we should be going now," Devin suggested.

"Good idea," I said.

"Liz," Jeff said with a grin.

Laurel and Marlon grinned as well.

We all walked towards the front door and walked outside to see them off since this was what my family did.

Suddenly, car lights came on down the street, and the car sped directly towards us as someone opened fire on us!

"GET DOWN! GET DOWN!" Marlon yelled!

We all screamed as we jumped to the ground and even tried to hide behind anything we could find as the car sped off into the night.

"What the fuck?!" I asked as I got up while I still tried to catch my breath. I looked over at Jeff; he was still on the ground. "JEFF!!!!!"

CHAPTER TWENTY-EIGHT

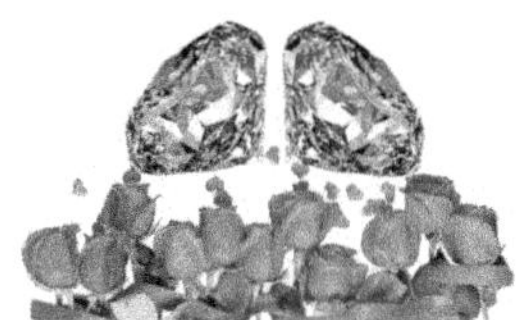

Nowhere in this neighborhood was there ever this much action as there was at this moment, as there were cop cars everywhere with their lights flashing as well as two ambulances here. Our neighbors heard the gunshots so someone had called 911 before all of us had a chance to do so.

Pilar was being checked out in the ambulance with Devin by her side as the cops continued to ask him questions. Marlon was being asked questions as well, as Laurel stood by him with Autumn's arms wrapped around her since the gunfire woke her up, and I absolutely hated that this happened. I felt that everything was my fault even though I knew it wasn't.

Jeff held me as we waited for the cops to get done questioning everyone else, and one of them approached us with something in his hands.

"Do these belong to either one of you?" he asked, as he held Jeff's glasses which had *one lens shattered by a bullet*!

"Oh, my God!" I said. "Jeff! Your glasses! They were hit!"

"Yeah, but I wasn't. Thank God," he said with a smile as he took them from the cop. He examined them. "Looks like I'm gonna have to get the lens replaced."

"That's an understatement!" I said, as I held up my right hand to my chest. "Jeff, what the hell? How were your glasses shot up but you weren't?"

"They flew off as I flew to the ground. Amazing shot from that car, I must say," he replied.

Marlon and Laurel came over to us with Autumn still holding on to Laurel.

"Are the two of you okay?" Marlon asked.

"No," I said, as I still wiped tears from my eyes.

Jeff smiled. "It's okay. I'm okay. She's upset that my glasses were shot up," he said, and showed his glasses to them.

"Damn!" they both said.

"You're a lucky man, Jeff. We all are since none of us were hit," Marlon said.

"You got that right!" Laurel said.

"Without a doubt," I said.

"Yeah, you're all right, I am; we all are. I thought I was hit at first that's why I stayed on the ground even after the car was completely out of sight. I checked myself and saw I wasn't and gave my many thanks," Jeff said as he still held me.

"Well, let me try and get Autumn back to bed. C'mon, baby," Laurel said.

"Good night, Aunt Lizzie and Jeff," Autumn said in her cute, sleepy voice.

"Good night, baby," I said with a smile.

"Good night, beautiful," Jeff replied as well with a smile.

Devin walked over to us. "How's everyone doing?"

"We'll survive," Marlon said with a smile.

"Speak for yourself," I replied.

They all laughed.

"She's gonna be okay, man. I got her," Jeff said.

"And his glasses got hit with one of the bullets," I informed Devin.

"For real, man?!" Devin said with genuine shock.

Jeff showed him his glasses. "Yeah, for real, man."

"Damn!" Devin said as he shook his head. "Someone was watching out for you tonight, man."

"For sure, man. I think we can all say that," Jeff said.

"Most definitely," Marlon said.

"Well, Pilar's going to the hospital just as a precaution, so I'm gonna get going so I can meet her there. I didn't expect any of this when we came over here, obviously."

"And it's obvious you don't know who did this, right?" I asked.

Jeff and Marlon looked at Devin to see what he was going to say.

"No, Liz. I don't know who did it. Sorry," Devin said. "See y'all later."

Hours later, Jeff and I laid up in his bed together. Especially since what'd happened hours before, I felt so safe being over his house and never wanted to leave here, and felt that whoever tried to shoot at us was obviously going after one of us, and I don't think it was Marlon and Laurel, it just happened to be their house that it happened at.

"Jeff?"

"Yes, baby?"

"Do you have any idea who could've been shooting at us like that? It's clear that whoever did that wanted one, some, or if not all of us, dead."

He shrugged. "I hope it wasn't me that they were targeting because I'm not into any shady shit, Liz, and I mean that. There's no reason for me to be. And since this has never happened at your home then it couldn't have been you, Marlon, and Laurel they were after, so that just leaves Devin and Pilar."

"Yeah, that leaves them most definitely. It was clear that they were followed to my house, and that's what scares me, Jeff. I don't want any shit like that to happen again. It's like one damn thing after another and I just don't want any more shit to happen, you know?"

"And it won't," he pledged.

"And how do you know that for sure?"

He shrugged. "I don't." He turned to me. "Liz. We can't go around living our lives in fear and in secret because yes, someone could very well be trying to ruin our road to the ultimate happiness. Now you saw me yourself tell everyone in that family room that you're the one who

I'm with and I don't have any secrets from you. As you know, Chrissie Lissette is crazy. I never had any kind of real relationship with her and I never will because I know what women like her are all about. However, I didn't think she would go as far as sending you nasty, secret texts and then telling the world of social media that I was engaged to her. You're the one I'm with because I knew a good woman when I saw you. I wanted nothing but fun with Chrissie."

"Well, that's not what she thought about the one-night stand the two of you had. She thought you were her man."

"Well, she thought wrong about that because I don't see how anyone can think a one-night stand is a relationship," he laughed.

"This isn't funny, Jeff. Something just doesn't feel right about what happened tonight. I'm glad everyone got their confessions out and as you see, Devin admitted we never had an affair."

"Then what is it that you don't feel right about?"

"That's just it, Jeff. I don't know. I just have a feeling that someone just doesn't want us together and as you see, they're still stopping at nothing to break us apart, if that was any indication about what happened earlier tonight. No disrespect to Devin and Pilar, as well as especially to Marlon and Laurel, but no one cares that they're together, so that leaves us, and it's obviously clear that people have a problem with us being together and like I said and can't seem to stop saying, they will stop at nothing to break us apart. I mean, this is the happiest I've ever been in my life and as you see, Pilar tried to ruin that when she sent you that picture of me and Devin because she thought he was cheating on her with me, and then you got that Chrissie Lissette who was the one sending me those texts and then reported a boldface lie to the media about being engaged to you? *Engaged?* What is the hold you have over women, Jeff?"

"No hold, Liz. They just need to realize that whatever I had with them was whatever I had with them and now it's over. Like I said earlier at your house in front of everyone, Chrissie and all the other ones need to accept the fact that I'm not interested in rekindling what any of us had because it wasn't anything, at least to me it wasn't."

"Well, it's clear that they felt differently."

"And that's not my fault because I doubt any of them would've felt any differently if I was some broke dude or even mediocre."

I grinned. "Can't disagree with you there."

He returned the gesture. "Exactly, Liz. And I felt like it took me a long time to find someone like you. Someone real, someone who is with me for the right reasons rather than for the wrong ones."

"And I wouldn't be with anyone for the wrong reasons because relationships like that don't last. I just never thought I'd be this happy again when I met you, and to think I almost lost you tonight . . . my goodness."

"And I could've lost you as well. All of us could've been killed tonight, and that's a scary thought. I think we'll eventually find out who shot at all of us, Liz. No one gets away with anything."

"I sure hope so."

He held me tighter and then kissed me on my forehead. "And do you believe Devin when he said he doesn't know who did it?"

I let out a deep sigh. "I honestly can't say that I fully do."

CHAPTER TWENTY-NINE

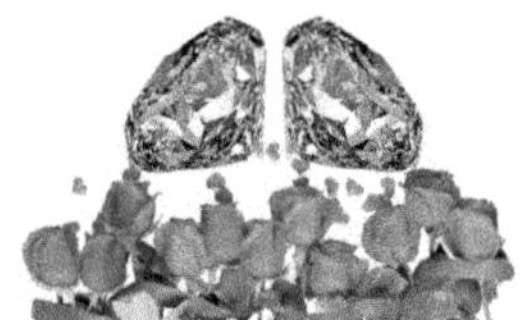

Chrissie Lissette freshened herself up while looking in her Too Faced compact. She put the compact down and then took a selfie.

Detective Maria Brady walked through the door of the interrogation room.

"So, Chrissie Lissette. You're the one who had the whole world thinking that you were the lucky woman engaged to billionaire Jeff Vick, huh?" she asked her as she pulled up a chair and sat down at the table across from her.

"Why are you bringing that up? What does that have to do with anything?" Chrissie asked, as she sat wearing a tight white cropped t-shirt and just-as-tight blue jeans. She swung her 40-inch braided ponytail to her back. "I'm not here to talk about that."

"Well, I know you're not, it's just that we have a history of you stalking Jeff Vick as well as his girlfriend Liz Green, so it was only appropriate to bring you in here for questioning in the drive-by shooting at Liz's home where she lives with her sister, brother-in-law, and niece. I don't think it was a coincidence that Jeff was there when this happened as well. Looks like your timing was perfect, but your aim wasn't, considering the fact that there were four other people out there who could've gotten hit by the gunfire."

Chrissie shook her head with a grin. "I'm not gonna sit here all day and let you try and convince me that I had something to do with trying to shoot Liz or Jeff, or both of them. Jeff is a jerk, okay? But that doesn't mean I wanted him shot. I honestly don't know what Liz sees in him."

"Are you only saying this because he chose to have her as his girlfriend and not you? Because he made it clear through his lawyers that he never had a serious relationship with you, Chrissie, and that your engagement to him was just as fake as that ponytail you're wearing."

She gasped in disgust. "Oh! So now you're gonna insult me? What does my hair have to do with anything? I really don't give a fuck about Jeff, okay? I'm a social media model. I can have any man I want."

Maria grinned. "Well, it's clear that you thought Jeff was the only man for you, and why would you say you were engaged to him if you didn't believe that yourself? He told us that you were just a woman he wanted to have fun with; he never wanted a serious relationship with you considering the fact what the two of you had was a one-night stand, and any idiot knows that's not a relationship."

She rolled her eyes. "Yeah, whatever. He's just talking like that now because he has a girlfriend. He's not gonna be with that bitch for that long. She doesn't look like nothing. He's just trying to deny our relationship, that's all, like he's done with all of the other women he's been involved with."

"Well, he admitted to the women that were his actual girlfriends, like a woman by the name of Karis, and some others from his past. He never mentioned you. Now you know that made you madder than hell, mad enough to wanna shoot up the woman's home who you feel took your so-called place."

"I don't know what the hell you're talking about, and like I said, I'm not gonna sit here in this shit-smelling room and keep going in circles with you over something I didn't do. I don't give a shit what Jeff says, we had a relationship. These motherfuckers always out here acting all new when they get a new girlfriend, and then wanna act like the past ones don't exist. Yes, I admit to texting him a lot because I felt he owed me an explanation because I felt that he did and I feel that he still does, but I'm not gonna get shit from him. I don't want him like that anymore anyway, but he can continue to take me on shopping sprees and fuck me and eat my pussy whenever he wants because I admit he's good at that shit, because he's the type who's incapable of seriously loving anyone, and Liz will soon find out what every woman knows about him, especially the ones who's been with him like me."

Maria continued to stare at her as she shook her head. "Where were you on the night that this shooting happened at Liz's home?"

"At home taking care of my kids; taking care of my business. I wasn't with any man or anything because I don't allow men around my kids. And why the hell would I shoot up people standing in a yard when one of them is a good friend of mine, and pregnant at that? Like I said, y'all need to let me go because y'all are questioning the wrong person. Yes, I was involved with Jeff, and that's always gonna be on him if he doesn't wanna admit that our relationship was way more than what it was. I don't care at this point. There're too many men out there to be worried about Jeff Vick. They may not be at billionaire status, but that's okay because I'll never run out of a supply of them."

"Well, if that's all true, Chrissie, then how come you have a record of nasty and threatening texts that you'd sent to Liz? We have a copy of them since she gave them to us when we told her we were bringing you in for questioning about this latest incident regarding her and Jeff. Would you like to see them?"

"What the hell for? I was just trying to warn her about him, that's all. Being with him is not gonna make her happy, and she should know that by now."

"And how is her happiness any of your concern? Because the texts weren't in any way, shape or form of you trying to warn her about him, Chrissie, they were of you harassing her; telling her that her relationship with him wasn't gonna last, asking sarcastically did she know where her man was—you know, harassing stuff that a scorned woman would send to another one that she wants to be like."

"I'll never wanna be like Liz. Fuck that shit."

Maria sighed. "You may go."

"So, what do you both think?" Detective Stanley Gold asked Jeff and me.

Jeff and I were here since they'd called us to come in and watch since they picked Chrissie up to be questioned about what'd happened at my house.

I shrugged. "I just don't know what to think. This woman stalked me and she stalked Jeff. And her saying she never wanted to be like me is the biggest shit lie I've heard, because if that was true then she would've left us alone from the start. She's just not to be trusted so I don't know why she was let go."

"We don't have anything to hold her on," Stanley informed me. "She doesn't have any outstanding warrants, nor do we have any hard evidence tying her to this crime. We can't keep her here."

"What about her texts to me? That was harassment!" I said.

"Why didn't you contact us earlier about it when you first started receiving them? You could've filed a complaint and we would've brought her in for questioning about it since Jeff did when she started harassing him. You didn't have to wait until today to bring it up and give us a copy of them," Stanley informed me.

"Because I didn't know who it was, that's why!" I angrily replied.

Jeff looked at me as I continued to stare into the interrogation room as Chrissie gathered up her things and then left. "Look, we didn't come here for *us* to be interrogated, okay? Liz and I just wanna know who shot at us that night. It has us both still on edge, as well as her sister Laurel and brother-in-law Marlon, as well as her ex-boyfriend Devin and his pregnant girlfriend Pilar."

Stanley grinned. "Wow, Jeff. That's pretty interesting. Whoever did this definitely could've been targeting the two of you."

I shook my head as I still sat in my seat staring in the now-empty interrogation room. "People just don't wanna see me happy; see us happy. Someone did this and they were directly targeting us. Now I don't know if that chick was telling the truth or not, but all I do know is that I don't care what the hell she says, I'm not ruling her ass out by any means. This bitch told the world a boldface lie that she was engaged to my boyfriend and as you see when she was in that room she *still* didn't wanna admit that she did it. I just think she lies a lot. If she didn't do the actual shooting then I still believe she had someone do it because there's no telling what a bitch like that would do and what she will do next."

Stanley looked at me and then looked at Jeff. "What do you think, Jeff?"

Jeff shrugged. "I don't know. But anything's possible." He got out of his seat and pulled me up out of mine. "We're gonna find out who did this, Liz. Whoever did this is not gonna get away with it."

I nodded with a smile. "I know." *But she probably already did,* I thought.

CHAPTER THIRTY

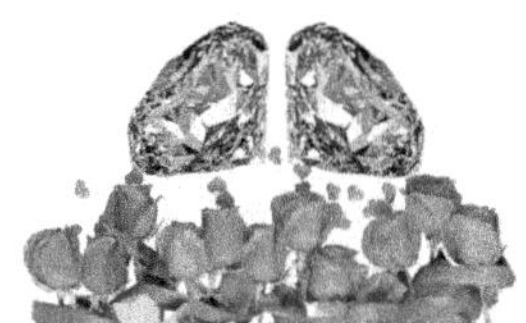

Later on that evening, Jeff and I sat in the suite area of his bedroom and watched a movie, but I don't think either one of us were really into it. We knew what was on our minds, and we both knew we would keep thinking about all of this until this person was caught. I still thought it was Chrissie Lissette—I didn't care what anyone said—it was just something about her, and I felt she simply got away with another thing that involved me and Jeff and was never gonna suffer the consequences for her actions.

"This movie is boring," I said, and then let out a sigh.

"It's not that bad, Liz," he said with a smile. "You wanna watch something else?"

"No, not really. I guess you're right; it's not bad. I just have a lot on my mind."

He picked up the remote and turned off the movie and turned and looked at me. "Talk to me."

I shrugged. "I just think a lot of shit has happened lately and it's just put a damper on our relationship. We're supposed to be happy and from the looks of it, it's clear that neither one of us are. Are you still happy being with me, Jeff?"

"Of course I'm still happy being with you, Liz. If I wasn't then I wouldn't be with you. I hate that you're so concerned about everything that's been going on lately. Look, we'll probably never find out who tried to shoot at us, and at this point I think we should just forget about it. We're one of the most fortunate couples out there and I wanna live like it again, not live in fear. Is that okay with you?"

I smiled. "Yeah, that's always okay with me. I'm sorry about being so concerned and everything, I just think we have something great and people will stop at nothing to ruin it."

"Well, they haven't ruined shit since we're still together, now did they?"

"Well, now, they almost did. I wasn't sure if we were still together after you thought I'd slept with Devin and said you needed your space. I thought during that time you found someone else."

"There was no one else, Liz. I just took some time to myself just like I said I was going to. If I met someone else during the time that we were taking a break from each other and thought she was someone I wanted to be with instead then how would that have made me look? I've never cheated on you since we've been together. You can even ask Jenelle if you want."

"I believe you," I said with a smile.

We kissed.

He looked at his phone. "I'll be right back."

Oh, no! Not this shit again! I thought. "Where are you going? Who is that?" I asked, as I got up as well.

This clearly was someone else since everything was out in the open about Chrissie Lissette, and I wanted to know who it was, and he was not leaving out of this room until he told me.

"I have to go to the bathroom, Liz. C'mon now, you can't hold me hostage from it."

"I'm not trying to hold you hostage from anything, Jeff. It's just that you always seem to get up and go somewhere out of my sight when you get a certain call or text. It's obviously not all of the time since you've gotten a ton of calls and texts while I've been with you, so I know it's always a particular text or call you receive that it's clear you don't want me to know about, and it's clear that Chrissie Lissette wasn't the only one."

"That's because it's none of your business, Liz."

My mouth dropped!

"It's none of my business, Jeff? *None of my business,* huh? How come it's none of my business? I'm your girlfriend and I've kept quiet each and every time you've done this since we met, with the very first time being when we were in your dad's treehouse the night of your parents anniversary. I just feel that we've been with each other long enough where you won't have any secrets from me."

"I don't have any secrets from you, Liz. And I don't remember going off when I got a call that night when we were in the treehouse."

"Well, I'm not gonna argue about it, Jeff, because I remember it like it was yesterday. And this is something you've been doing constantly in my presence since. It's clear that there is someone other than Chrissie Lissette. I lost count of the times we were together when you'd gotten a call or text and you ran off because it's clear you didn't want me to know who it is. What the hell is going on?"

"Nothing is going on, Liz, okay? You just need to know that I'm with you and only you. That's it. Now, will you please excuse me because I need to go to the bathroom for real, I'm not kidding."

I watched him as he walked away from me with his phone still in his hand as he texted this person back. I waited until he got out of my sight. I grabbed my purse and headed home.

"He said it was none of my business," I said, as I wiped tears from my eyes as Laurel sat down a mug of hot tea in front of me.

She sat down across from me. "Well, you tried, Liz. I just think it was very risky to ask him who it was, and that's because—"

"It's none of your business," Marlon reconfirmed to me, and then took a sip of his drink.

"Marlon!" Laurel said.

"I hate to say it, but it's true. And I warned you about asking him, Liz."

"Yeah, I know you did, okay? I didn't forget. It just came out. I knew it wasn't Chrissie Lissette, so I know it's someone else."

"And it's still none of your business like he said, Liz," he reconfirmed once again. "And then you walked out on him when you didn't get your way. You're acting entitled, and that's not good at all," he informed me.

Laurel stared at me as she sipped her tea.

"I don't think I was acting entitled about wanting to know about something that he's clearly been hiding from me for months because it's clear there's someone else in addition to Chrissie. Sure, we all have secrets, but when he's constantly getting up and walking away from me completely out of my sight then it's obvious to me he doesn't want me to know who keeps calling and texting him. I just think I have a right to know. I've been with him for months."

"Women who have been with their men for years know their place in their relationships, Liz. That's what you have to learn, especially with someone like Jeff. You know he's the one percent of the one percent, and you don't wanna lose someone like him for thinking you're entitled to know about everyone who's calling or texting him when you're together," he said.

I sighed as tears still streamed down my eyes. "We've just been through so much it seems. We still don't know who shot at all of us that night, and now he's acting as if something as simple as a text is none of my business. Maybe everything is none of my business."

They looked at each other.

"Why are you saying it like that?" Laurel asked.

"Well, I don't wanna be that girlfriend who's always left in the dark about everything. You all think it's so great being with someone like him but now you both see that it's not all what people think it is."

"It's better than being single and knowing you'll never have a man like him, Liz. And that's over ninety-nine percent of women. You beat the odds in a tremendous way and it's like you don't even realize it. I'm being harsh with everything I'm telling you because this is how a lot of men feel, but you have a man who's on a whole other level, a level that almost all of the men in this world aren't on and will never be on. All I gotta say is, don't get comfortable being with him, Liz, and you asking him who texted him showed him that you were," Marlon said.

"I just felt I had the right to know who it was and why he had to get up and leave while he responded to that person. I just wanted to let him know that I noticed a pattern with him doing that since I've been with him. I think I've been quiet about it long enough."

"And that should be the last time you ask him about it, Liz. Being quiet about things that are none of your business is not always a bad thing, especially in this case with you being the girlfriend of a black billionaire," he said.

I sighed. "Jeff is human before he's black and especially before he's a billionaire. It's just—"

"HEY! GET THE FUCK OUT OF HERE!" a man's voice yelled from outside.

We all jumped out of our chairs and ran outside to see what was going on.

We watched as a car sped down the road and disappeared into the night.

I turned and looked our driveway. "WHAT THE FUCK?!?!?!?!?"

CHAPTER THIRTY-ONE

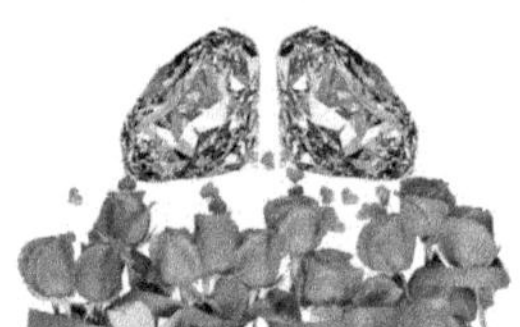

"Damn. This is really fucked up. I'm sorry this happened, Liz," Jeff said, as we all stood back and stared in shock at my $128,000 beautiful white Porsche Panamera completely destroyed with black graffiti spraypainted all over it and the words "BITCH" and "WHORE" written all over it, as well as all four tires being slashed.

I shook my head. "Any bright ideas of who could've done this?" I asked, as I watched the cops take pictures of my car and collect evidence.

"No ideas, Liz. I'll get you another car."

"Don't bother," I replied, as I still stared at the car.

"What?" Jeff asked.

Laurel and Marlon looked at me as if I was crazy.

"Why bother getting me a new car when she's just gonna do it again," I said.

"Who's gonna do it again?" Jeff asked.

Laurel and Marlon looked at me to see what I was going to say.

"Chrissie Lissette. Who do you think?" I said in a calm manner, because at this point it was not gonna do any good to yell and scream about something and someone who was not gonna leave me alone; leave us alone.

"Yeah, it was quite possibly her since she was pissed off about being questioned about the shooting here not too long ago, so you're probably right. Have you made anyone else mad?" Jeff asked.

"Have you?" I asked, as I tried not to get angry.

"Liz, calm down," Laurel warned me.

"No, I haven't, Liz. Look, I don't wanna fight about this. I said I will buy you a new car if you want."

"And I'm declining it because what if she just does it again? And again and again? I'm sick of this shit, Jeff. No one wants to see us happy and our relationship succeed. They just wanna keep us down where they are. This is really stressing me out and I just don't know how long I'm gonna last before I end up lashing out at everything."

"And I don't wanna see that happen," Jeff said. "We'll find out who did this, Liz, and I guarantee you it won't happen again when this person is caught."

I shook my head. "I can only hope so."

But in reality, I was very doubtful. I never had these kinds of problems in my past relationships. Never. This was all on a whole new level and I knew it was all because I was with Jeff. But things didn't have to be this way and I was determined not to have them this way, and I was gonna do whatever I could to make sure nothing like this was ever gonna happen again.

"Wow. That Chrissie Lissette is something, isn't she?" Karis asked, as she breastfed her daughter.

"Yeah, she is. But she's trash. All she can get is those thirsty-ass simps and she knows it. She's way below the level that Jeff would consider girlfriend material to him, that's why she was only some play chick to him for one night, and he even admitted it," Chloe said.

"I know she is. It's just funny to me that everyone thinks I'm the one who shot at all of them that night and now they think I did this as well? Well, I proved that I didn't do both. Of course I feel that one day I'll get

Jeff back, but I know that's not the way I'm gonna get him back. Only psychotic bitches like Chrissie Lissette would do the shit she's doing to get someone back that she never had to begin with. I'm just gonna sit back and watch all of this because it's very entertaining to me."

"And that it is," Chloe said. "I just don't know why women like her think she deserves Jeff so much. I have to admit, even Liz is on a higher level than her."

"But Liz is not on a higher level than me."

"Oh, absolutely not! And she will never be. There's a reason why these things keep happening to her, Karis. It's because it was never meant to be between her and Jeff, and when they both finally realize it, you can step back in your original place with him and be a couple once again."

"And I can't wait until that day."

CHAPTER THIRTY-TWO

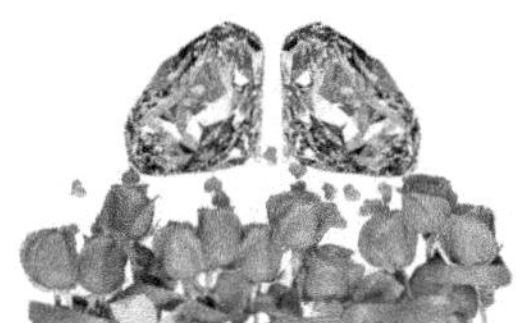

"So, I don't have to explain to you why you're here—or do I?" Detective Maria Brady said, as she sat down in the interrogation room.

"Yeah, you do, because I don't know why the hell I'm here. I'm already sick of this."

Maria shook her head. She opened a folder and took out a piece of paper. "Well, you're here because there was a compact—a pretty damn nice compact at that—found at the crime scene of Liz Green's car being vandalized. The DNA on the sponge matched your DNA," she informed her, and slid the paper over to her.

"I don't need to see it. Those tests are not always accurate."

Maria reached over and grabbed the paper back from her. "Well, it looks like you got some explaining to do, and it's not just about Liz's car being vandalized, it's about who did the shooting at their house as well."

"I don't know why I'm in here for any of this shit. I didn't do a damn thing."

"Well, it's too bad because your DNA says otherwise. But before I go on, what's your real relationship with Jeff Vick? Because as you know, Jeff had girlfriends, and you weren't one of them."

"Look, I'm very well aware I was never Jeff's girlfriend, okay? I don't need to be reminded of it. But Jeff and I had a different relationship compared to all of the other girls. I don't give a shit about the others, all I care about is how he treats me, and he still treats me very well."

Maria looked confused. "What do you mean by he still treats you well? You're still seeing him?"

"Yes, we are still seeing each other. This shows you he's never been serious about his past girlfriends nor the present one."

"But it's clear that he's still with Liz. And what you've done to try and get him to be with you and only you is very criminal."

"I don't know what you're talking about because I didn't do anything. Jeff caused all of this mess, not me. He always told me he was looking for love yet he had it right with me, but he didn't realize it that's because he didn't wanna admit that I'm the only one for him and he still doesn't. He's always trying to look for something better when it wasn't gonna get any better than what he had with me. He acts like he doesn't want me as a girlfriend because I got kids and he doesn't want a pre-made family; said it's just a bad deal for a man, especially a man of his status—so stupid."

"Nothing stupid about that. It's his preference and you and other women have to respect it, not do what you did. You took it to the extreme to try and get rid of someone who he's with now who had nothing to do with your alleged relationship with him. Now you're looking at some serious time because of it."

"I'm not looking at any time. There's no way anyone can actually a hundred percent prove that I did these things. Yeah, I love Jeff, but that doesn't mean that I would go to these extremes."

"Does he love you?"

She lowered her head. "Does it matter?"

Maria shook her head. "Yeah, I would say it does. Because what woman who has kids by other men would do something like this to try and trap a man who doesn't love her, doesn't have kids by him, and a man who has never made her his girlfriend? Sounds insane, don't you think? And it's really insane to think that doing the things that you did that you're gonna scare his girlfriend so much that she's not gonna wanna be with him anymore. You see how they're still together despite what you did."

"But probably not for long! Look, I know you've never been with a man like Jeff Vick. He's like no other man out there. I know he loves me, he's just too afraid to admit it; too afraid to show his real emotions. Despite him being with Liz, we have always stayed in contact—what does that tell you?"

"Nothing," Maria replied.

"Well, it's something to me because if it wasn't he would've totally ignored me after he met Liz. He doesn't love Liz, he loves me, and it's all a matter of time before he admits it to me."

"And it's clear you will do anything for love and to destroy the happiness of others, huh?"

"I didn't destroy anything. I just want my man for me and only me, that's all."

"Oh, and before I forget to tell you, there's proof that you did this shooting," Maria said, as she pulled out another piece of paper. The gun that was used in the shooting was found in your house, and your fingerprints and DNA match the fingerprints and DNA on it. You're looking at some very serious time."

"I don't wanna answer any more questions. I want my lawyer now."

"Okay, that's fine that you lawyer up, but you're still being booked for the things you've done. So stand up, Beverly, and put your hands behind you back."

We all stared at Jeff as we sat in the interrogation room. It was Laurel, Marlon, Jenelle, and Detective Stanley Gold.

"Beverly. One of Karis's best friends. You were screwing around with her, too. What the hell has gotten into you, Jeff?" I said.

"This is all my fault, Liz, and I'm sorry," Jeff said as his head hung low.

"Sorry? You could've gotten us all killed that night because this crazy bitch was obsessed with you and you kept seeing her even after you met me? Were you seeing her when you were with Karis?"

"No, I wasn't. I started seeing her when Karis and I broke up. I told her not to tell her about us," he replied.

"But Karis knows now," Jenelle informed us as she grinned while looking at her phone. "She's blowing up social media with her madness. Needless to say, she says this is the ultimate betrayal and Beverly is no longer a friend of hers. You really caused some shit, big brother."

"But Beverly caused even more. I had always been more attracted to her than Karis, and after Karis and I broke up, one thing just led to another. But I told her because of Karis, I could never have her as my girlfriend and didn't want her as my girlfriend anyway. And then I met Liz."

"Have you seen her since we met?" I asked.

Everyone looked at Jeff.

"Yes," he confessed.

"YES?!" I yelled.

"Calm down, Liz," Laurel said.

"Jeff, how the hell could you?" Jenelle said.

"Please, everyone, hear me out," Jeff said.

"We're listening," Marlon said with a serious look on his face.

Jeff held on to my hands. "I only saw her when we were in our period of separation, Liz. That's it. I told her we needed to talk, she came over my house, and we did just that, talk. I told her I was still with you and wanted to stay with you and that she needed to move on because we were never gonna be together like the way she wanted us to be. I never told I loved her; no shit like that. Grant was there. He can vouch for everything I'm saying. Nothing else happened."

I nodded, but I didn't know what to believe. "I believe you," I said anyway.

Everyone nodded with a smile.

Jeff still held on to my hands. "Liz, I honestly didn't think I would ever meet anyone like you. I just didn't think it would happen and happen so fast. Yes, I was secretly seeing Beverly at the time even though Karis was trying to get back with me. I just kept talking to her through texts and on the phone just trying to explain to her that I really liked you and that she needed to move on."

"So she's the other one you were always jumping up and going off out of my sight to talk to, huh?"

"Yes, she's the other one," he finally confessed. "But it's over now, Liz. We can officially get back on the right track, and I wanna do that, but I need to know that you're with me on this."

I stared at him. I honestly didn't know what else to think. All of this was just a big, hot fuckin' mess that never seemed to have had an end to it . . . but now I felt like it finally did, and I could only hope that it stayed this way. "Yes, I'm with you."

Everyone smiled.

"Great. And to celebrate being back on our road to ultimate happiness, I wanna know if you wanna have a date tomorrow at my house? A dressy date, so wear a beautiful cocktail dress for me."

"It's a deal."

We kissed, and it felt different . . . in a good way. I could feel all through the kiss that all of this was behind us now and that we could finally move on, and I couldn't wait for our date tomorrow.

CHAPTER THIRTY-THREE

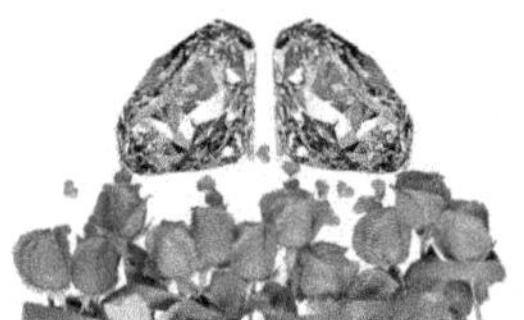

I walked down the beautifully lit walkway on the way to Jeff's treehouse, and walking there was like walking to his dad's treehouse on our very first date. I smiled as the beautiful black wrought iron fences were decorated with beautiful red roses, as well as there being red rose pedals on the ground as I walked in a beautiful $8,745 Dolce & Gabbana beautiful light pink strapless dress embellished in tonal feathers and had a flare thigh-high hem. I smiled as I still made my way to the treehouse while I stared down at my Dolce & Gabbana crystal shoes. I felt so beautiful in this look; exactly like the way I felt when I went on my very first date with Jeff, and we ended the night in his dad's treehouse. So much had happened since then and I wanted to put it all behind me, especially behind us, tonight, and from the looks of how he set up this date, he already had.

I reached the treehouse, but Jeff wasn't in sight. "Jeff? Where are you?" I walked inside the treehouse that was even bigger than his dad's. It literally looked like a small house. I walked back outside . . .

And my whole family, as well as Jeff's, was waiting for me!

"What the?!" I said, as I tried not to swear, especially in front of Jeff's parents and Jenelle, as well as mine. "What are you all doing here?"

Jeff appeared! "Hello, Liz. I hope you don't mind them all being here." He had on a sharp dark navy suit and was actually wearing a tie.

"No, we don't mind!" Laurel said, as she held on to Autumn's hand.

"We sure don't," Marlon said with a smile.

Everyone laughed as they nodded in agreement.

"No, of course I don't mind you all being here, I just thought this date was gonna be with Jeff and me only. But I am glad to see both families here," I said. I looked at Jeff. "What is going on?"

He took both of my hands. "Liz, I didn't mean to catch you off guard with all of this, but we've been through so much in the months since we've known each other, and I feel you have stuck with me through it all. I messed up a lot, and it takes someone very special to see my flaws and believe that I can get better, and I'm getting better. I'm getting better because after everything that's happened, Liz, I found the love of my life, and I knew it the first time I laid eyes on you at that concert. I honestly didn't think a woman like you existed anymore."

A man came out of nowhere and handed Jeff a box.

And he got down on one knee!

Everyone erupted into applause as I erupted into tears!

"Liz, there is no one I wanna spend the rest of my life with other than you. Will you marry me . . . *now*."

Everyone looked at each other and shrieked with joy!

I had to take a second and process what he'd said.

Marry him.

Now.

"Right now?" I asked, as tears flowed from my eyes.

"Yes. Right now," he replied with a smile as he was still on one knee.

I took a deep breath. "Yes. I'll marry you right now."

Everyone erupted in cheers as he slipped the beautiful and flawless 15-carat marquis-shaped solitaire diamond ring on my ring finger. It was so beautiful it looked fake.

Suddenly, two tall, gorgeous men seemed to have appeared out of nowhere, and they looked very familiar. They were wearing the same type of suit. They smiled at me and nodded as they made way for . . . .

"Oh, my God! *Dray Royce*!" Laurel said in shock. "I think I'm gonna faint!"

"And I'm not gonna catch you if you do," Marlon said with a grin.

"What's up, everyone? Don't want anyone fainting now!" Dray said with a laugh as he held hands with his wife Eve.

Everyone laughed as I stood in shock as the other black billionaire in Jeff's age range was standing right here along with his beautiful wife. They were the most stunning, most beautiful couple I'd ever seen and this was my first time seeing them in person. And now I knew the two men who were with them were their personal bodyguards, Auer and Leon.

"Hey, Dray and Eve. Thanks for coming on such short notice," Jeff said, as he shook hands with them as well as gave them each a hug.

"We wouldn't miss it," Dray said with a big smile.

"We sure wouldn't," Eve replied as well with a smile.

"This is my fiancee for a few more minutes, Liz Green," Jeff said with a smile.

"Very honored to meet the two of you," I said as I shook each of their hands.

"Thank you, Liz. Very nice to meet you as well," Dray said with a smile.

Lord, he is so gorgeous up this close and smells so good, I thought. But Jeff was my man, and I just couldn't believe I was the one he asked to marry.

Now.

"Nice to meet you as well, Liz. And we have *a lot* to talk about, and you know what I mean," Eve told me with a smile.

"And I look forward to it," I let her know.

A minister came out from nowhere it seemed, and in just a few short minutes, we were married.

I was officially married to Jeff Vick.

I thought I was dreaming.

Never did I think a date was gonna turn into a marriage proposal, and not only a marriage proposal, into a very unexpected wedding. I had no reason to object to this. I felt we'd been through enough since we'd met and we were officially on our next journey together. All we needed was who we had right here with us to witness a true love that I felt for him right from the start, and he felt it for me as well.

"This wedding has gone viral already!" Marlon said with a smile as he looked at his phone.

"Like I knew it would!" Jenelle said with a smile.

"Devin just sent his congratulations to the two of you, and wanted you to know that Pilar just gave birth to a healthy baby boy a few days go," Laurel said.

"Tell them we said congrats as well," Jeff said with a smile as we held each other. I nodded with a smile.

"Oh, and speaking about babies, I'm *not* pregnant," I informed everyone.

"Are you sure?" Marlon asked.

"Yes, Marlon! I'm sure!" I said with a laugh.

"She's not. I don't want you all to think I wanted to marry her today because of that reason," Jeff confirmed with a smile.

Autumn ran up to me and wrapped her arms around my waist. "Aunt Lizzie! You're married! Does this mean you're a real princess now?"

I held on to her hands. "Of course, baby. And remember what I said about princesses. Any woman can be a princess as long as she has a man who loves her and treats her like one, and I have that man," I said as I looked at Jeff with a smile; he nodded back with a big smile.

"My wife and I wanna go on a walk. We'll be back in a little while," Jeff said.

"Take your time, Mr. and Mrs. Jeff and Liz Vick," Laurel said with a big smile.

Moments later, we were walking down the walkway with our arms around each other.

"What are the odds of this happening to a woman? *Wow,*" I said, as I looked at my wedding ring.

"That's why I wanted it to be a 'date' you would never forget," he replied with a smile. "I can't believe it. We're married, Liz. I honestly didn't know what you were gonna think of me asking you to get married now. That's the part I was very nervous about."

"Yeah, I can tell!" I said with a laugh. "I didn't know you even planned on proposing to me, but then you were like, forget an engagement, let's do this right now!"

He laughed hard. "It's how I do things! No one has ever done that before in my family, and I just felt that I've already built something for my future wife, so I felt there was no need to waste time with an engagement."

"I agree. And you saying that you've already built something for me is an understatement. And yes, I am all for the say-I-do-and-keep-it-moving route. I have no need to show off with a wedding that costs out of this world just because you're a billionaire. I love what we just did because it shows the both of us the true love we have for each other. All we needed was our families here to witness our true love and that's it. Did they know about the proposal?"

"Not at all. I told them it was gonna be a party instead of a date like what we originally planned for when we were at the police station. I bought your ring a few weeks ago. I had it specially made so it took a while to get here."

"It's the most beautiful ring and biggest freakin' diamond I've ever seen. I can't believe I'm wearing this and it's a wedding ring, not an engagement ring."

"And I meant everything I said back there, Liz. I fell in love with you the moment I saw you at that concert. It was truly love at first sight. I said, 'I know that's my future wife, I just have to convince her of it.'"

"And you've convinced me, all right!"

We laughed once again.

"Oh, and I'm glad you set the record straight about not being pregnant. I didn't even think about that when I asked you to marry me and wanted to do it now. I know a lot of them were thinking that, they just didn't say anything."

"Yeah, I know they were, that's why I said it!" I said as I laughed.

"And I confirmed it." He looked at me. "And we can take our time, Liz. I'm in no rush. With everything we've been through, our new journey starts now. We have the world at our feet. I was looking for love and I found it, and I didn't think I would ever find it so fast to tell you the truth."

"And all I was looking for was to be happy again, and words just can't describe how happy I am now that we're married. I know we don't know what the future holds, but we're gonna take the chance and find out because we're going into it together. If we got through the shit we got through when we weren't married, then there is nothing in life we can't get through now that we are married."

"Exactly right, Liz. Life is a journey, no doubt, and it's how we handle the things that get thrown our way and we handled everything very well; we didn't let anything or anyone break us apart. We survived the first storm in our journey, and I admit almost all of it was my fault, but now we have a brand-new start. I want us to be together forever, Liz. I know that sounds cliché, but I mean it. The things that happened to us since we met happened for a reason, and like I said, it shows us that we didn't let any of it tear us apart. To me it shows us that we are meant to be together."

Tears welled up in my eyes once again.

"You're right, Jeff. This beautiful walkway filled with these red petals and roses on the balcony represents our new journey to live our best lives, and like you said about me, I don't see me spending the rest of my life with anyone other than you. There was a reason why I went to that concert that night even though I didn't wanna go; my future husband was there, even though I didn't know it at the time. You're not just one-in-a-billion, Jeff, you're once in a lifetime. And I got my once-in-a-lifetime man . . . forever."

"You sure do," he replied with a smile. "I love you, baby."

"I love you, too."

We kissed, and he swept me up off of my feet—just like how he swept me away with all of those roses he gave me the night we met—and carried me back to where everyone was as the song "Happiness" by The Pointer Sisters played over the speakers.

Happiness was not guaranteed to anyone. It was something we all had to work for, it something to strive for. It was also something people would obviously lie for, and even worse, try and kill for. Everyone wished they had it, but not everyone did nor did everyone deserve it, but for those who did, it was something to never give up on. Happiness never has a straight path to it, there are always twists and turns, but when it's finally achieved, it's worth everything that one had to go through to get it. Nothing in the world meant more to me than reclaiming what was lost for so long, and now what was lost was now found and in the best way possible with the best man possible, and it will be cherished forever.

ABOUT THE AUTHOR

Sheila Murdock is a combination of her birth name and her late grandmother's maiden name on her mother's side.

When she's not writing, she enjoys watching movies and TV shows - old and new - on YouTube, Netflix, and Amazon Prime Video, but always loves a surprising show she can find on cable TV. She also enjoys reading all kinds of non-fiction, but has a particular interest in African-American historical and contemporary non-fiction, but will read an occasional fiction book. She enjoys listening to old-school/throwback rap, hip-hop, and R&B, and jazz music from any era.

www.ingramcontent.com/pod-product-compliance
Ingram Content Group UK Ltd.
Pitfield, Milton Keynes, MK11 3LW, UK
UKHW021909190726
13853UKWH00002B/583

9 798227 693716